TUFF FLUFF

The Case of Duckie's Missing Brain

SCOTT NASH

CANDLEWICK PRESS
CAMBRIDGE, MASSACHUSETTS

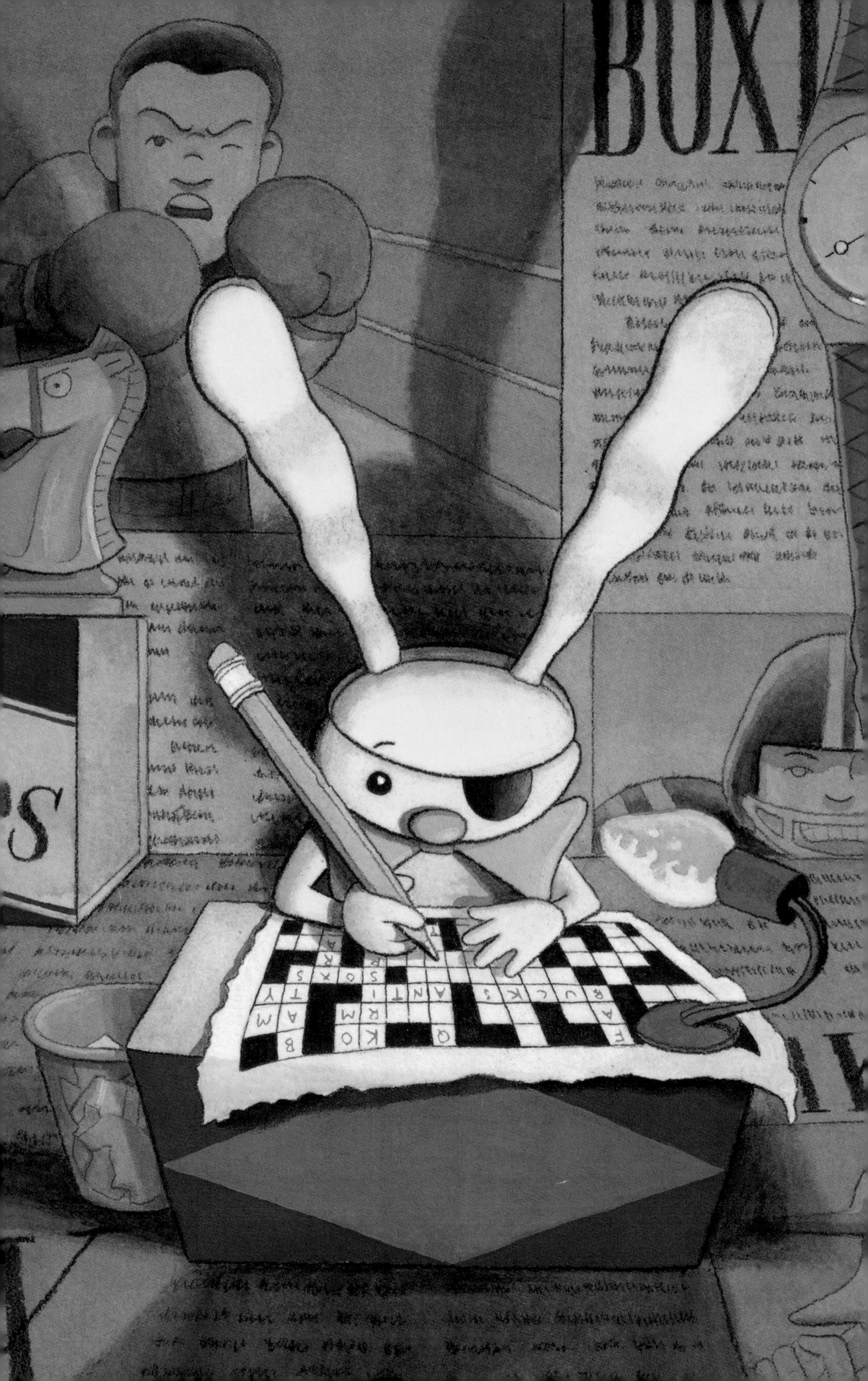

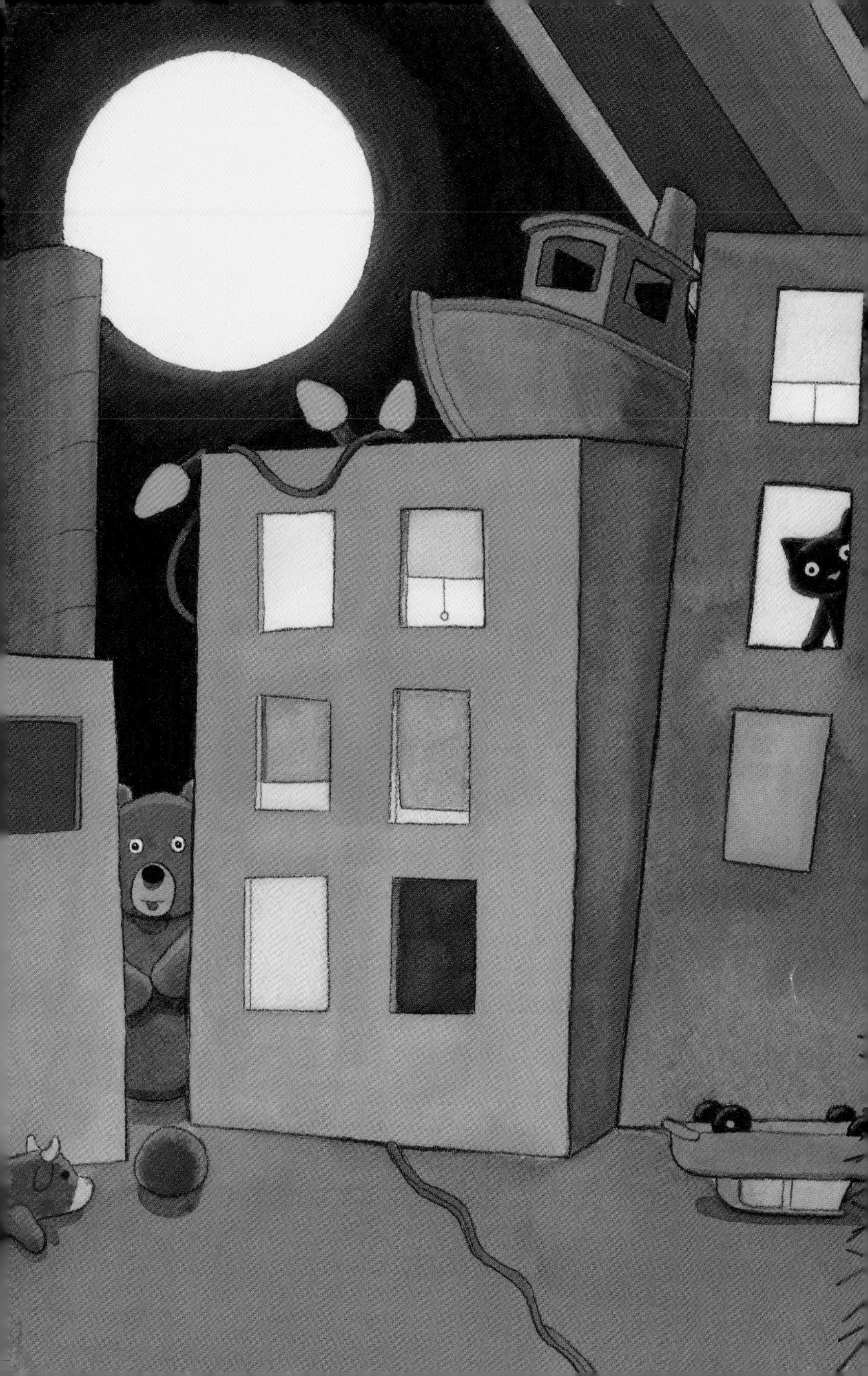

With heartfelt thanks to Mary Lee Donovan,
Ann Stott, and Nancy. And to my friends whose
beloved pals appear within.

Copyright © 2004 by Scott Nash

First edition in this format 2008

The Library of Congress has cataloged the original edition of this book as follows:

Nash, Scott, date.
Tuff Fluff: the case of Duckie's missing brain / by Scott Nash. —1st ed.
p.   cm.
Summary: When Duckie, a terry cloth duck, loses his brain and can no longer tell
stories to the other toys, Tuff Fluff the private investigator must solve the case.
ISBN 978-0-7636-1882-7 (original hardcover)
[1. Toys—Fiction. 2. Storytelling—Fiction. 3. Mystery and detective stories.]
I. Title.
PZ7.N17355Tu   2004
[E]—dc21   2003051629

ISBN 978-0-7636-3483-4 (small-format hardcover)

10 9 8 7 6 5 4 3 2 1

Printed in China

This book was typeset in Clichee and hand-lettered by the author.
The illustrations were done in gouache and pencil.

Candlewick Press
2067 Massachusetts Avenue
Cambridge, Massachusetts 02140

visit us at www.candlewick.com

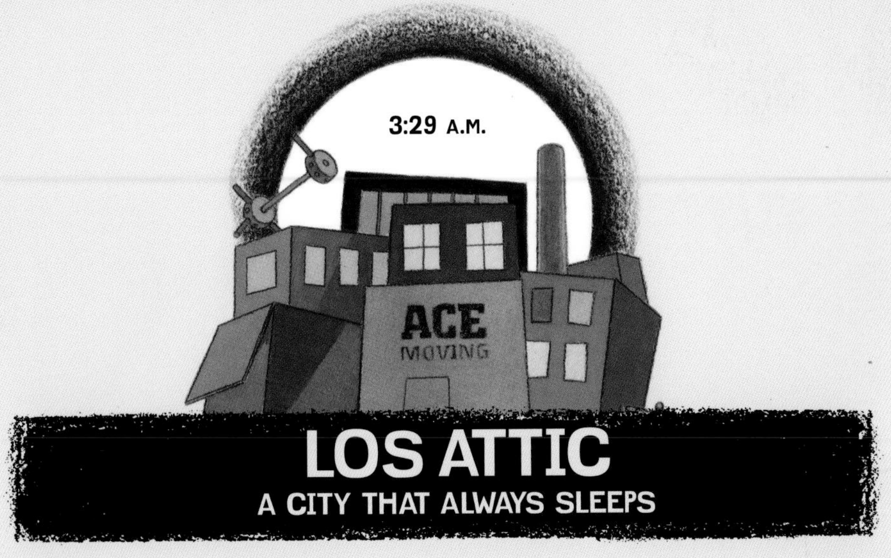
3:29 A.M.
ACE
MOVING

LOS ATTIC

A CITY THAT ALWAYS SLEEPS

My name is Flopsy Flips Rabbit. But nobody with any sense calls me that. To them I'm Tuff Fluff, Private Investigator.

It all started when I was sittin' in my office in the Ace Moving Box, workin' at the *Times* crossword puzzle. The watch on the wall said 3:29 A.M. It always said 3:29 somethin'. I was lookin' for an eight-letter word for *fake medicine* that begins with a *Q* when I heard a soft thumpin' at my door.

"It's open!" I called.

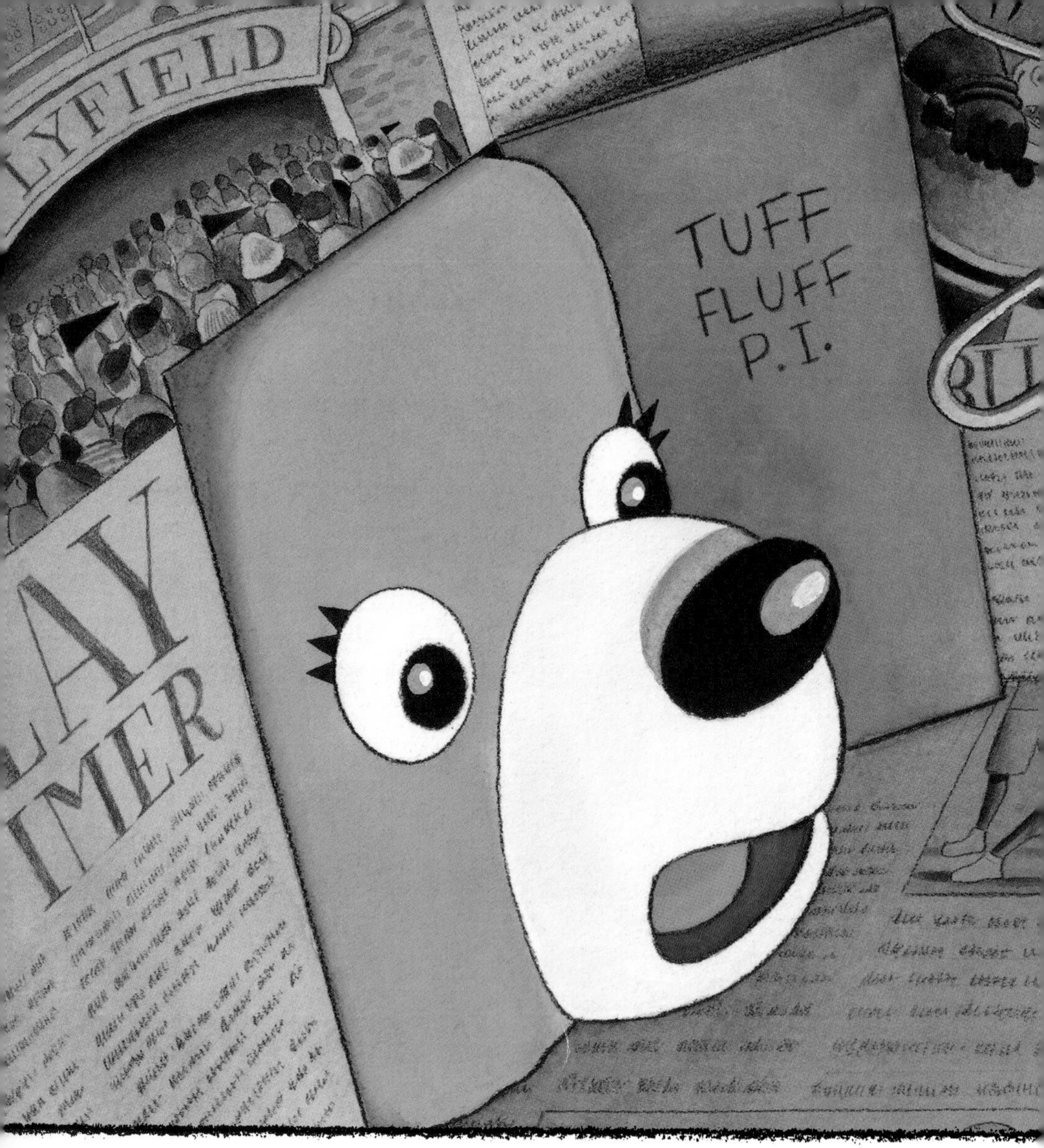
LYFIELD
TUFF
FLUFF
P.I.
LAY
IMER

I looked up to see who was there and found myself starin' right down the business end of a fuzzy muzzle.

"Excuse me, Mr. Fluff?" said the muzzle in a voice as thick and smooth as catsup.

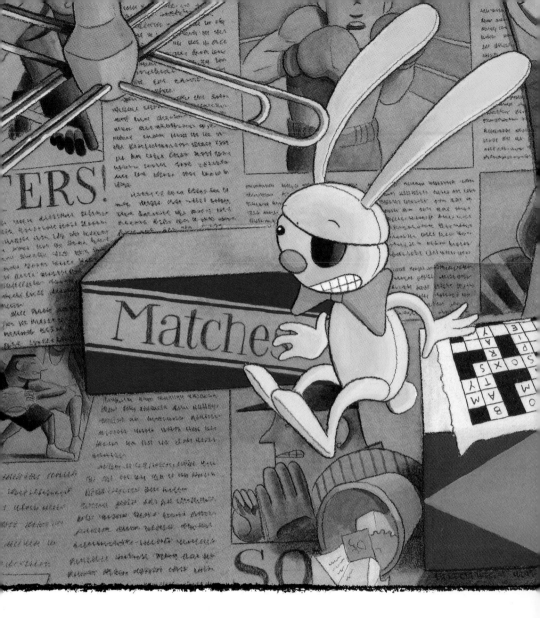

"That's me!" said me. "So what's *your* name, big stuff?"

"My name is Bluebell. I need your help! Something terrible has happened. Could we please talk . . . outside?"

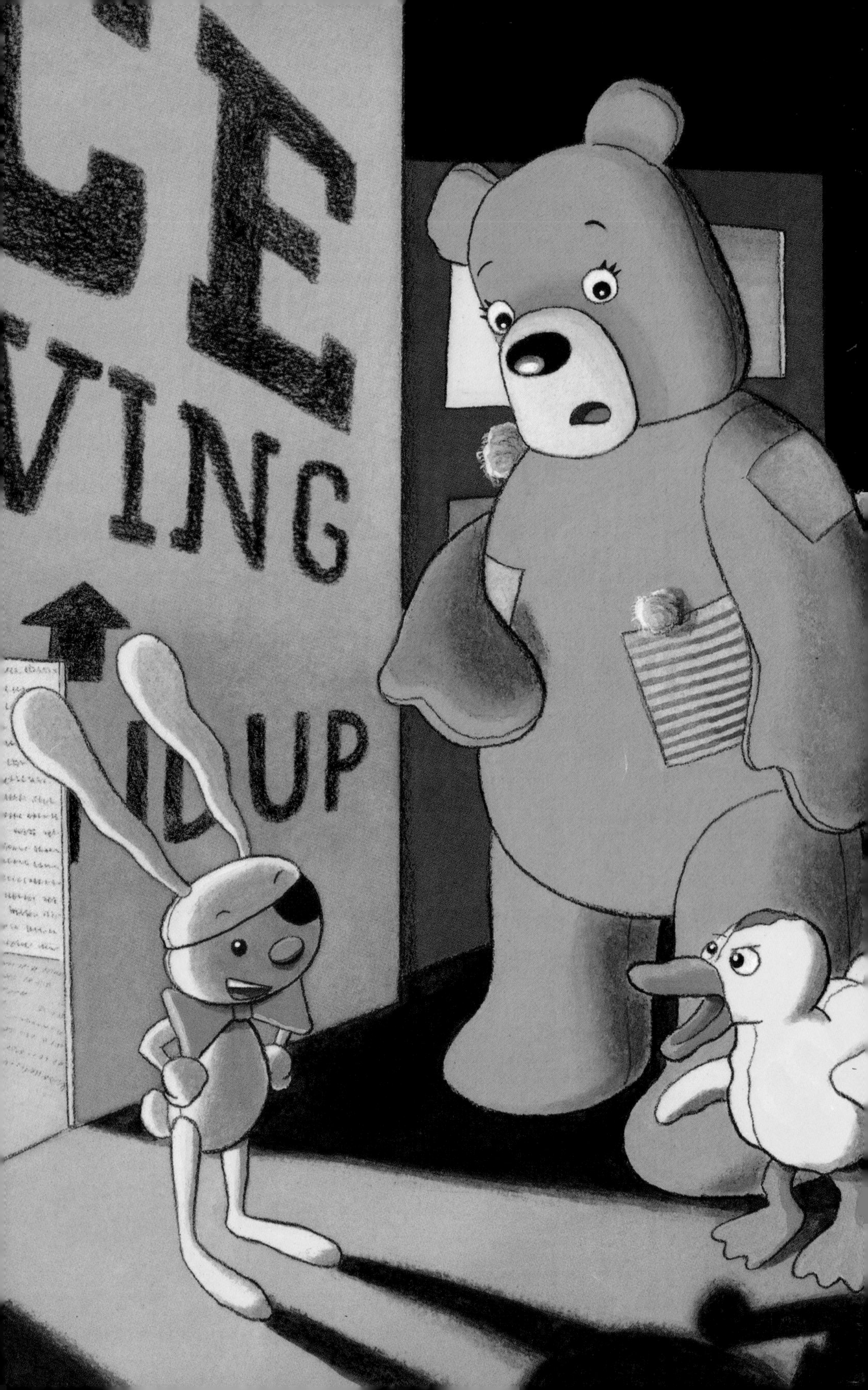
CE
VING
UP

I stepped outside to find that the muzzle was attached to the tallest teddy I'd ever seen. She was as big and blue as a whale in a room full of oranges.

"Okay, Big Stuff, what's the problem?" I asked.

She says, "My friend Duckie isn't ducky."

Something moved in the bear's shadow. Then out into the light stepped a yellow terry cloth duck.

"QUACK!" said the duck.

"Hmmmm. Seems pretty ducky to me," I said.

"But listen to him! All he does is quack," said the bear.

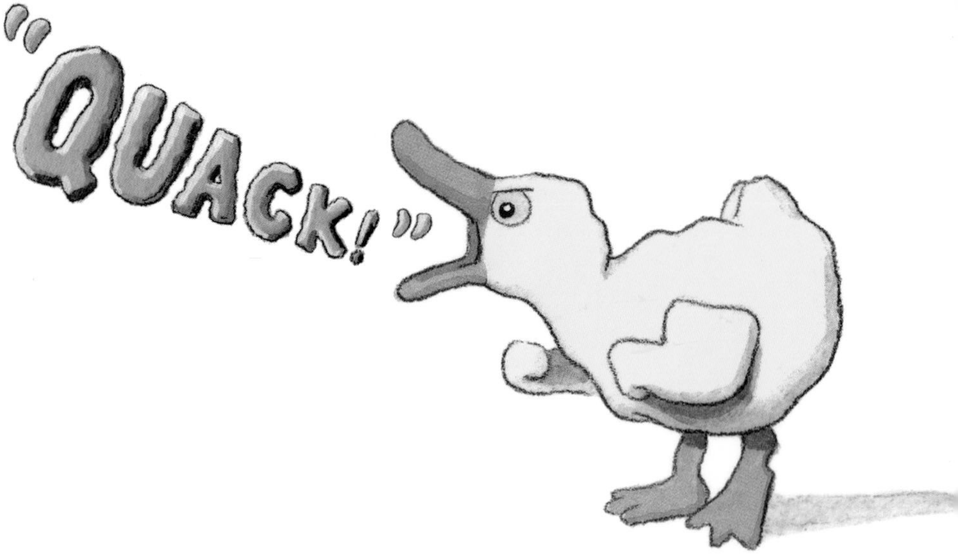
"QUACK!"

"Come here, Big Stuff," I said. "I wanna tell you a secret." She bent down close, and I whispered into her velveteen ear, "He's a duck, sweetheart. Ducks quack."

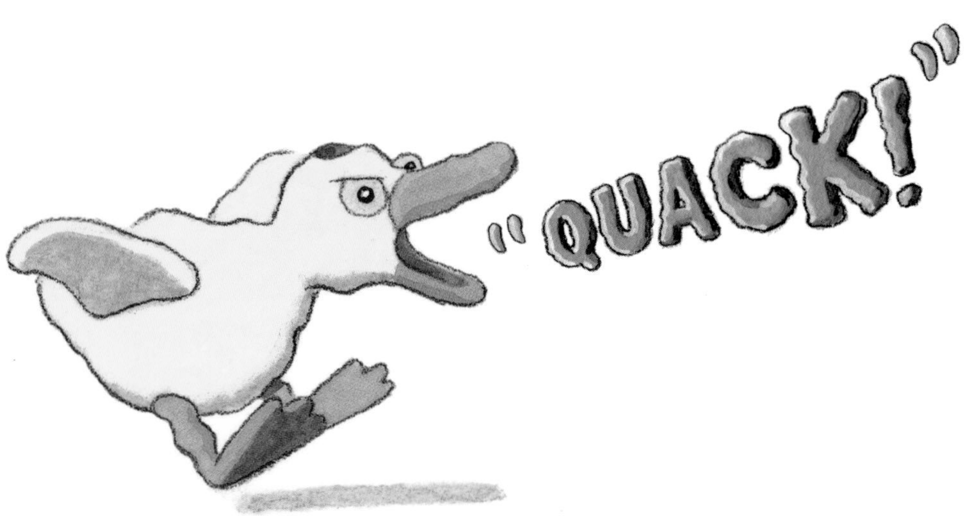
"QUACK!"

"I beg your pardon," the bear said politely, "but stuffed ducks don't quack. They talk, just like you and me. My friend Duckie used to talk all the time."

"**QUAALK!**" squawked the duck.

"I got it, I got it! But I'm a detective, not a doctor!" I said.

"Mr. Fluff, I beg you, please take a look at my friend."

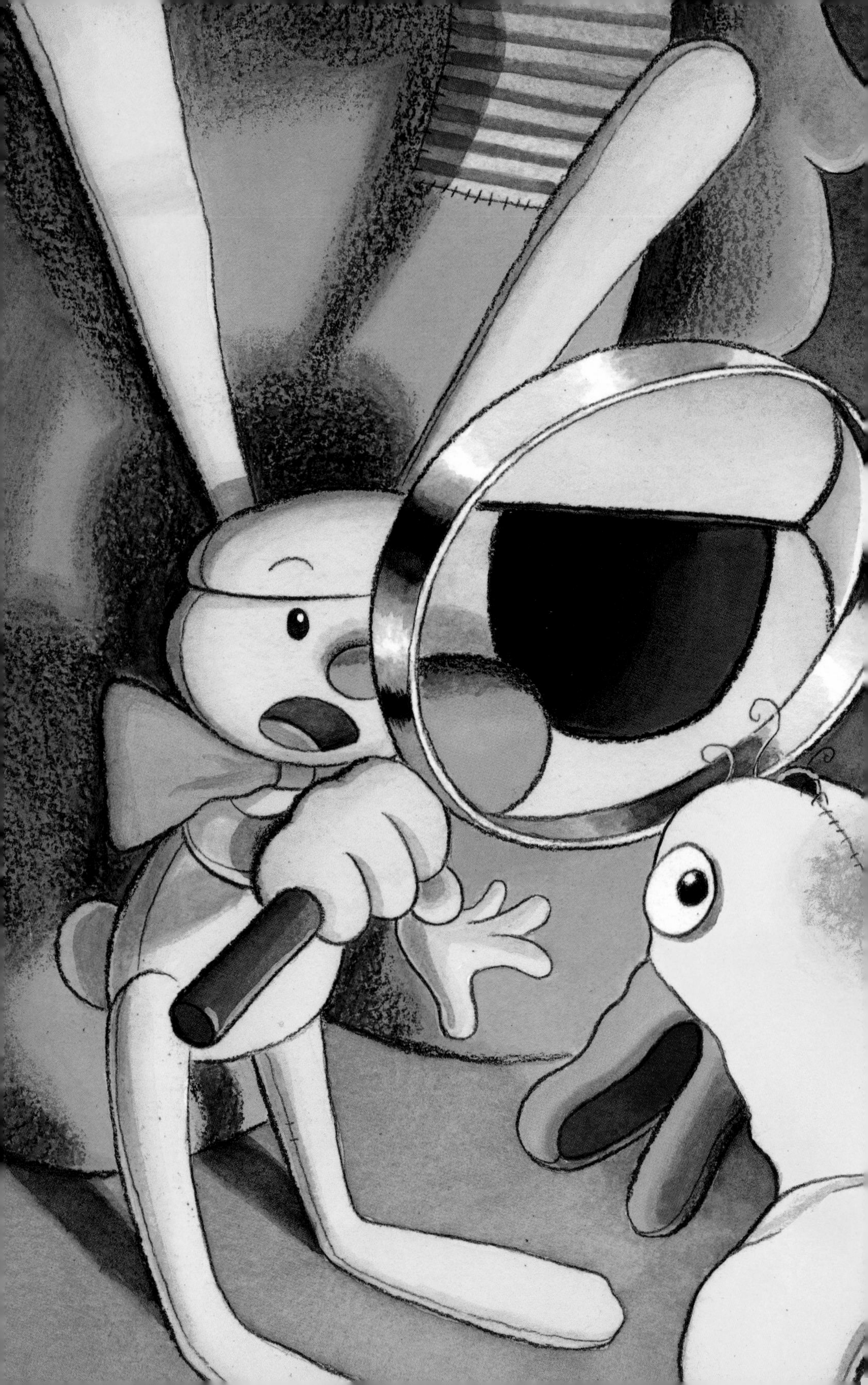

"All right, all right, I'll take a look," I said, as I pulled out my magnifying glass and inspected the duck from toe to head.

There at the top of the poor duck's head was a split in the stitching and a dark gaping hole.

"Someone's been playing foul with this fowl," I said. "His brain's been lifted."

"You mean

STOLEN?"

she asked.

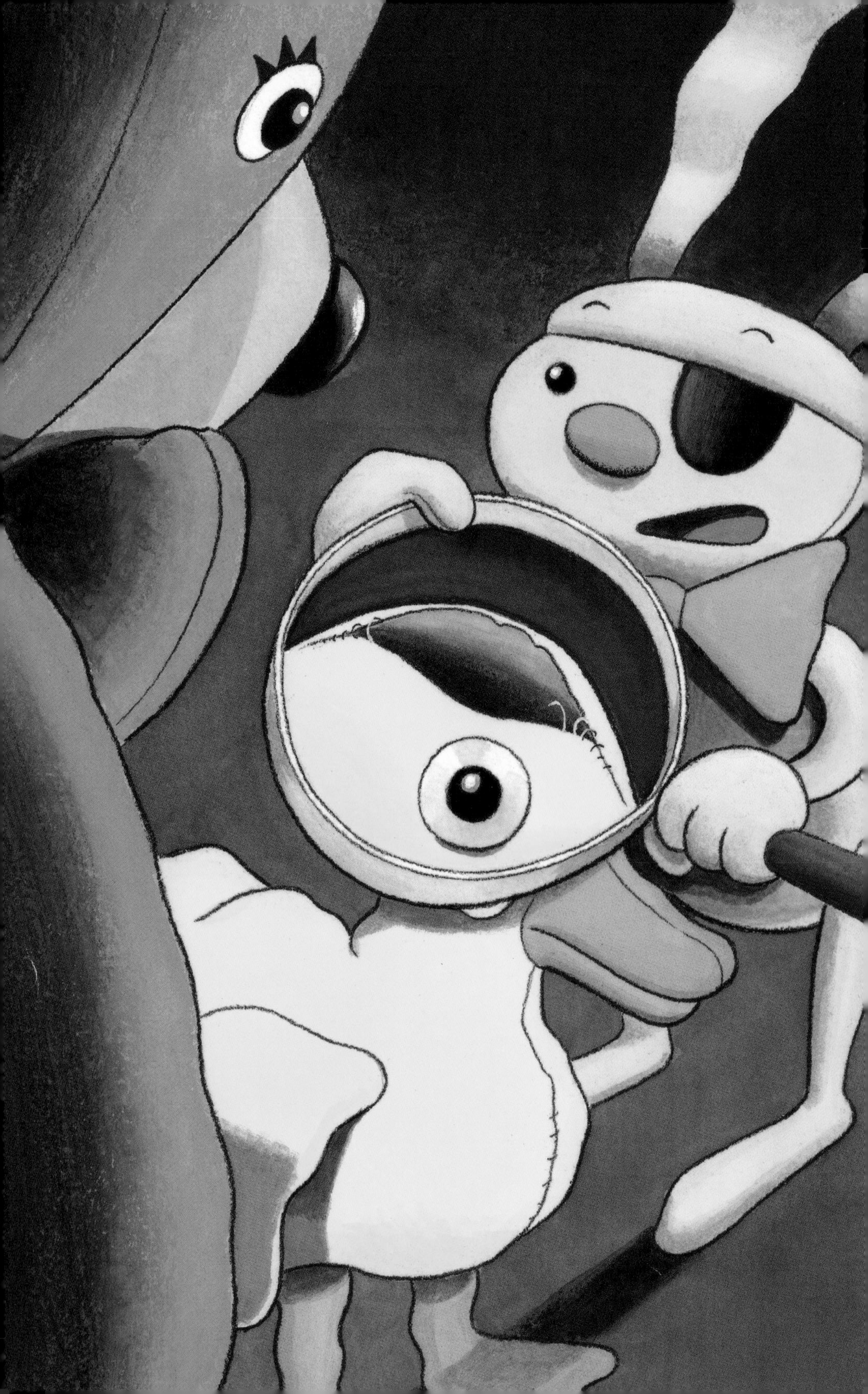

"Bingo!" I says.

"But who would do such a terrible thing—and why?" (I could tell she was about to pop a stitch.)

"Relax, Ursa Major. I'm a detective. Before we can figure out the who and why, we need to investigate the where and when."

I locked the door to the office. "We gotta visit the scene of the crime. Take me to Duckie's place."

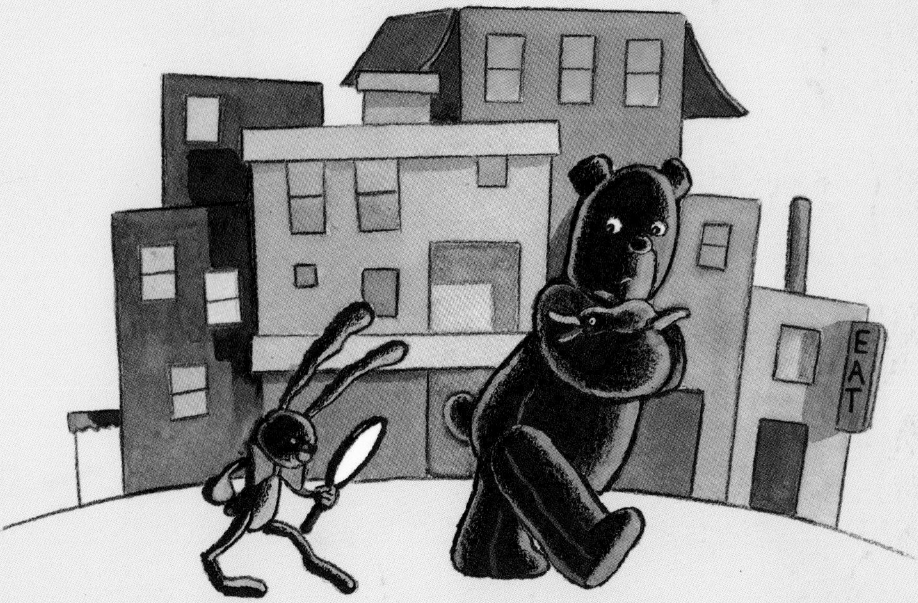
EAT

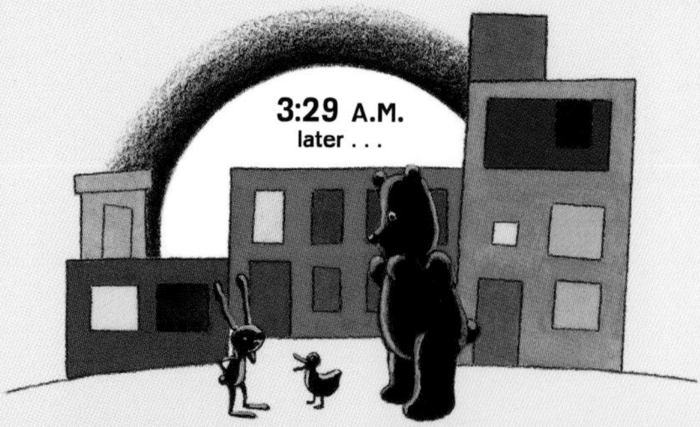
3:29 A.M.
later . . .

TO DUCKIE'S PLACE

We walked past noisy wind-ups, plastic action figures, and construction sets to Duckie's apartment box. It was a nice place on a quiet dead-end street bordering Beantown, the fanciest neighborhood in Los Attic.

"I'm too big to go inside. I'll wait out here," said the bear.

"Good idea! You stand guard and watch the apartment."

The entryway to Duckie's building was clean and well lit. So was the stairway.

I counted four names on the door buzzer, including one Justin Duckie.

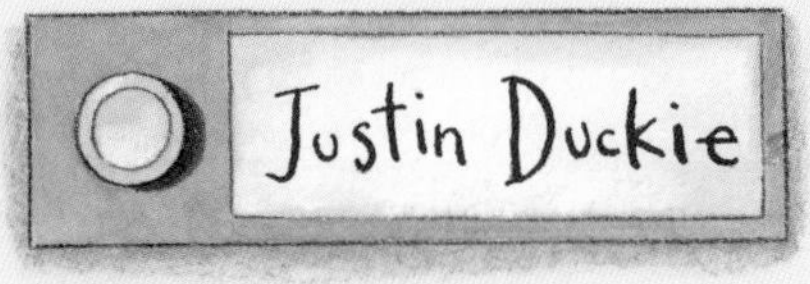
Justin Duckie

"What floor?" I asked, as we began climbing the stairs.

"Quird!" said the duck.

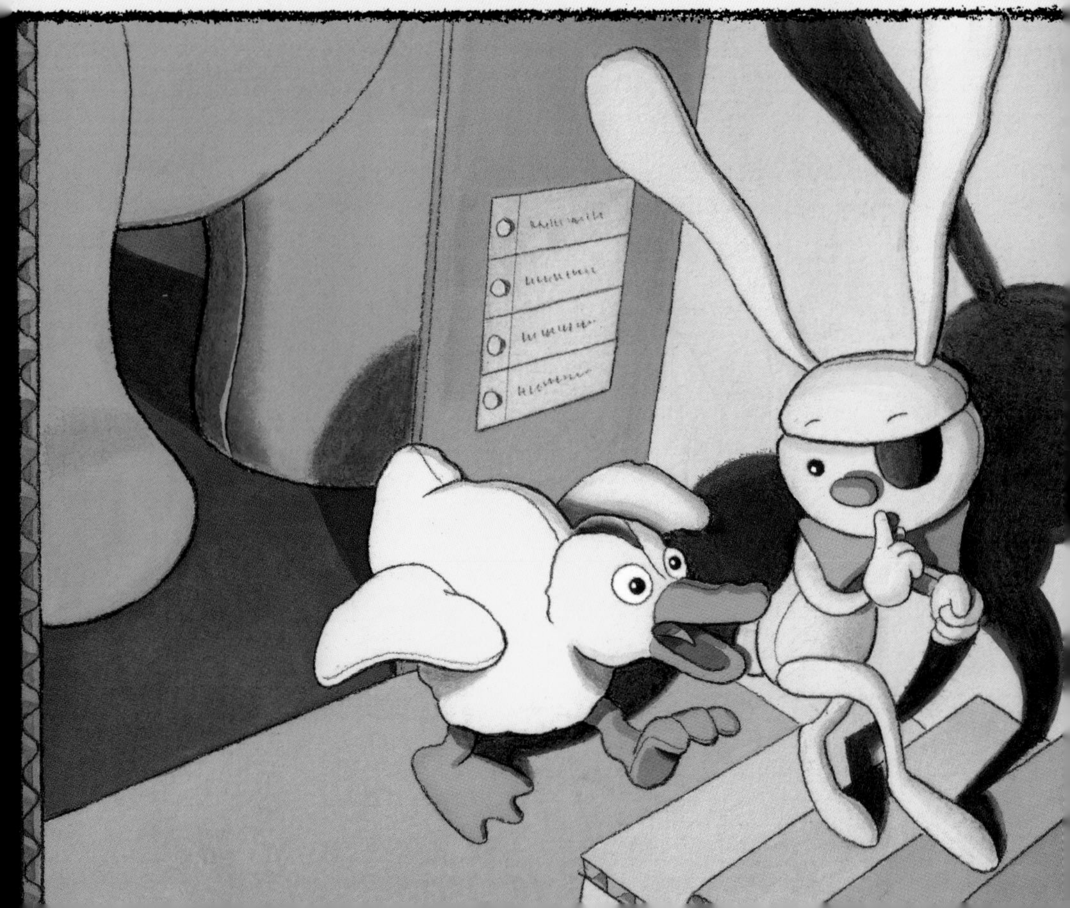

When we reached the second-floor landing, there was a CLICK and the lights went out. I set my feet and my fists, ready to knock the stuffin' out of anything that attacked. The landing shook as something came barreling down from the third floor and streaked past us, screamin',

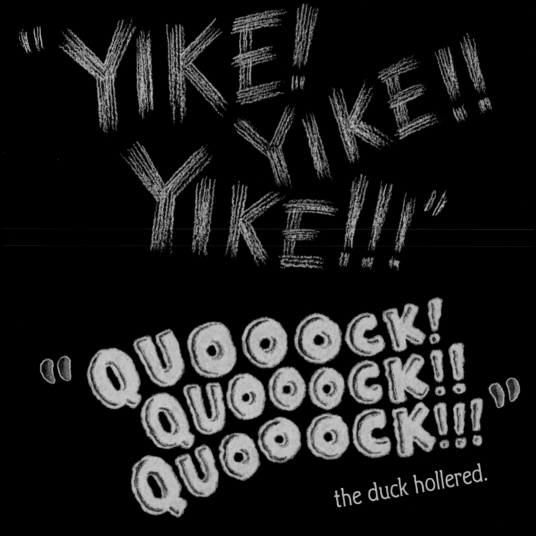

"YIKE! YIKE!! YIKE!!!"

"QUOOOOCK! QUOOOOCK!! QUOOOOCK!!!" the duck hollered.

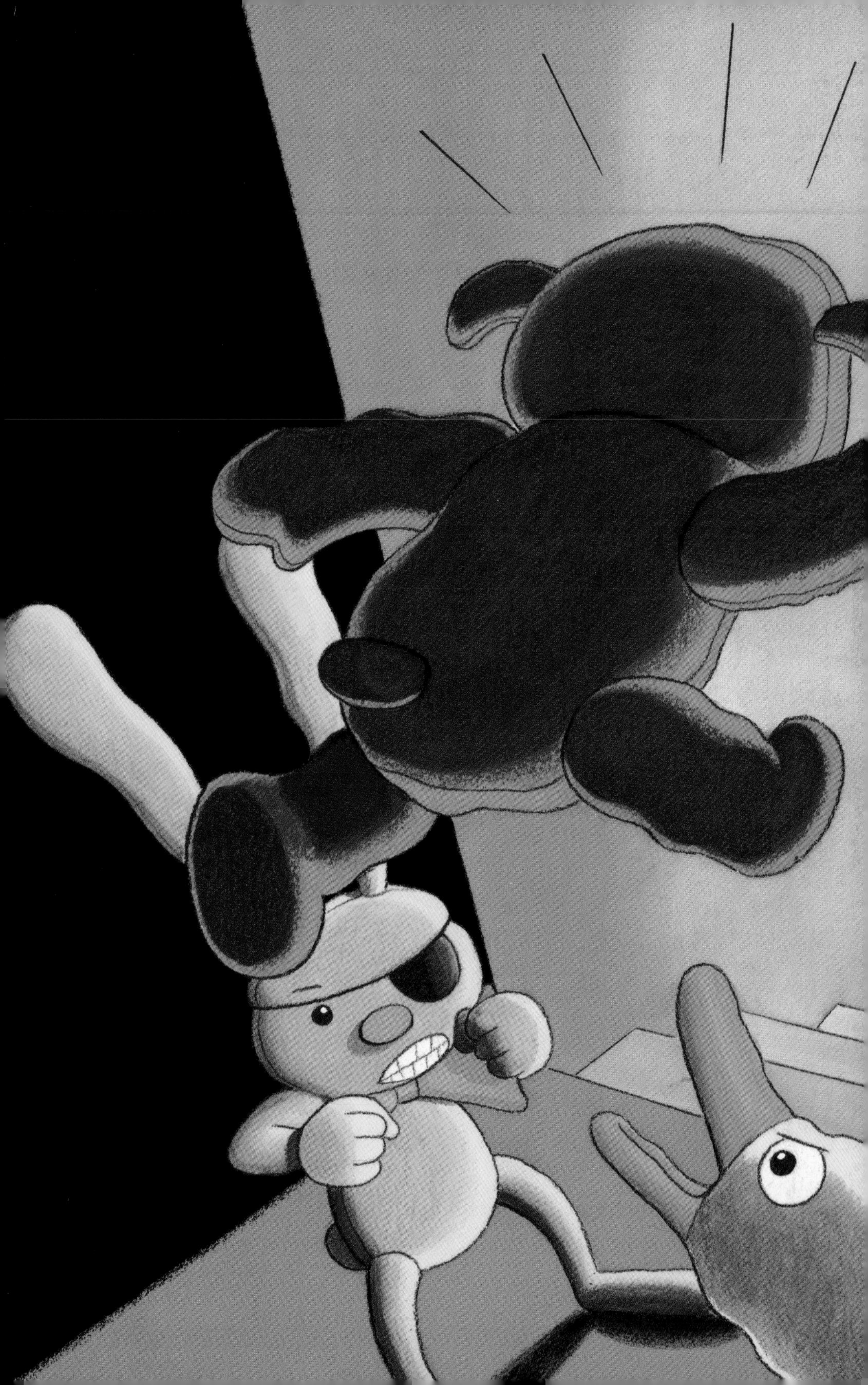

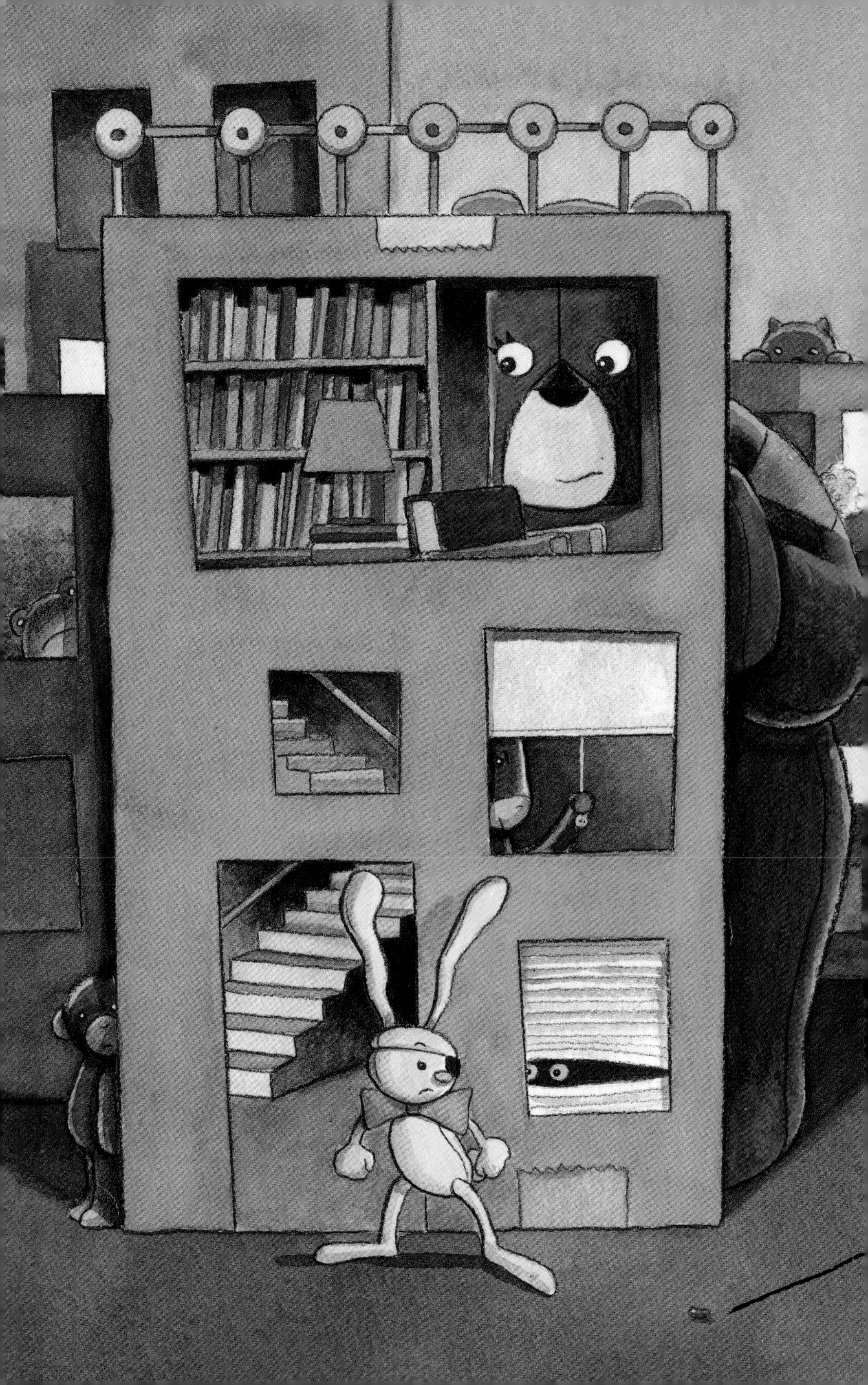

I gave chase, but whoever it was had already slipped out the door and disappeared down the street. Big Stuff seemed to have disappeared too, which was a good trick for a three-story-tall bear.

Just then I noticed somethin' on the ground. I picked up the evidence with a handkerchief. "A bean!" I murmured, and tucked it safely in my pocket. Then I ran back upstairs.

Duckie's apartment was a big place on the third floor with great views of Los Attic.

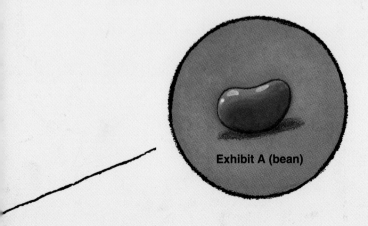

Exhibit A (bean)

"Big Stuff!" I says. Then I see Bluebell's face, peekin' at us through the window. "Where have you been?"

It turns out that the bear had been there the whole time with her face squished halfway in through a window at the side of the building, waiting for Duckie and me to enter the apartment. So she'd missed all the excitement.

The apartment was full of books from floor to ceiling. "For a fella with no brains, you're pretty bookie, Duckie!"

This seemed to snap Duckie out of his stupor. He pulled a book off the table, threw it on the floor, and began quackin' angrily at it. Poor guy.

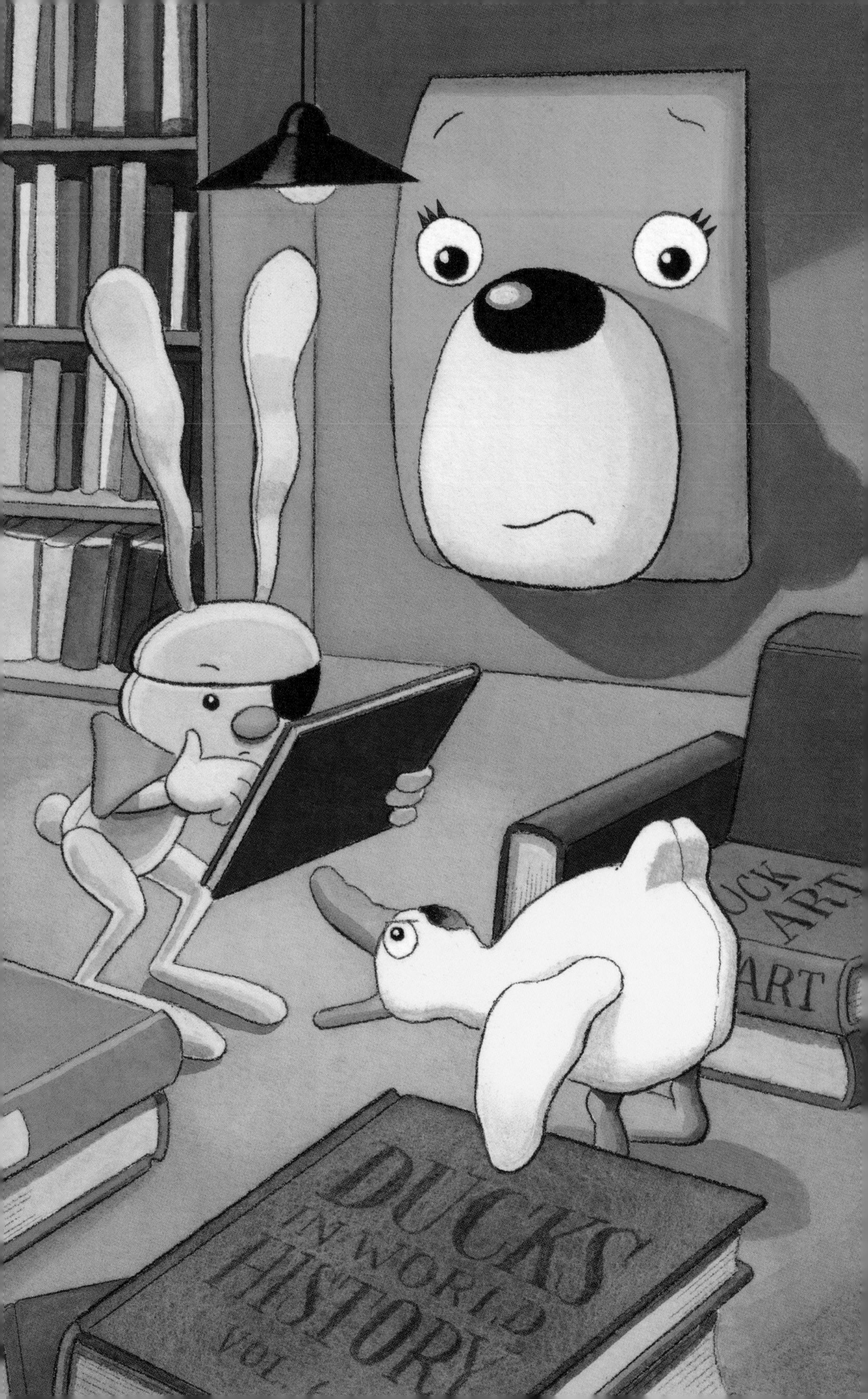
UCK ART
ART
DUCKS
IN WORLD
HISTORY

I picked the book up. It was a swashbuckler called *The High-Seas Adventures of Blue Jay the Pirate.*

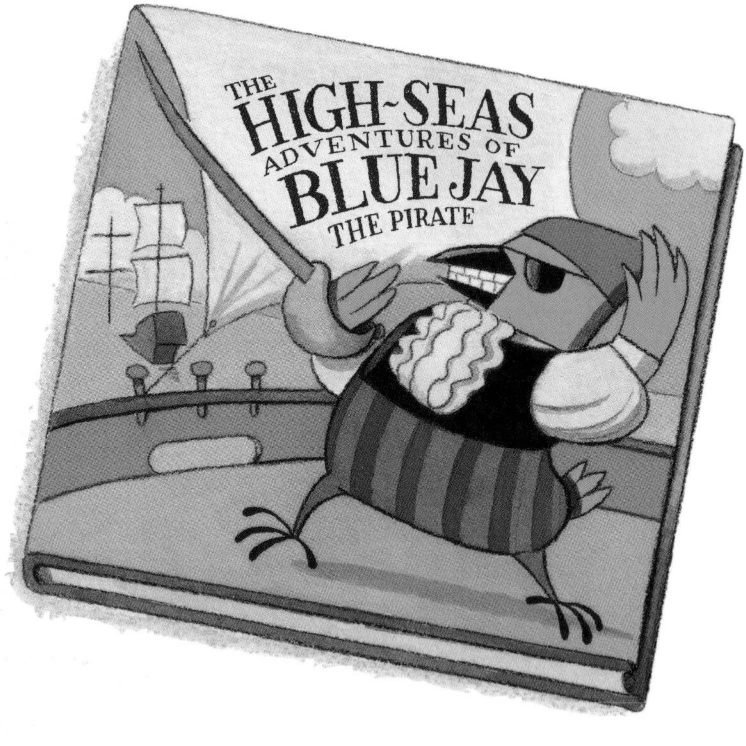
THE
HIGH-SEAS
ADVENTURES OF
BLUE JAY
THE PIRATE

"We're not gonna find the answer to this case in a book," I said, as I put the book back on the table. "Let's find the beanbag that rolled past us and see if he spills."

And with that we ventured into the heart of Beantown.

3:29 A.M.
later still . . .

BEANTOWN

There was no love lost between beanbags and
stuffs. To the beans, stuffs were riffraff, the old
toys. To us, beanbags were simply the newest
batch of castoffs. As we walked down the
street, we could feel the stares of itty-bitty
beanie eyes watchin' our every move. Big Stuff
cradled Duckie in her arms. The duck glared at
something or someone up ahead and growled.

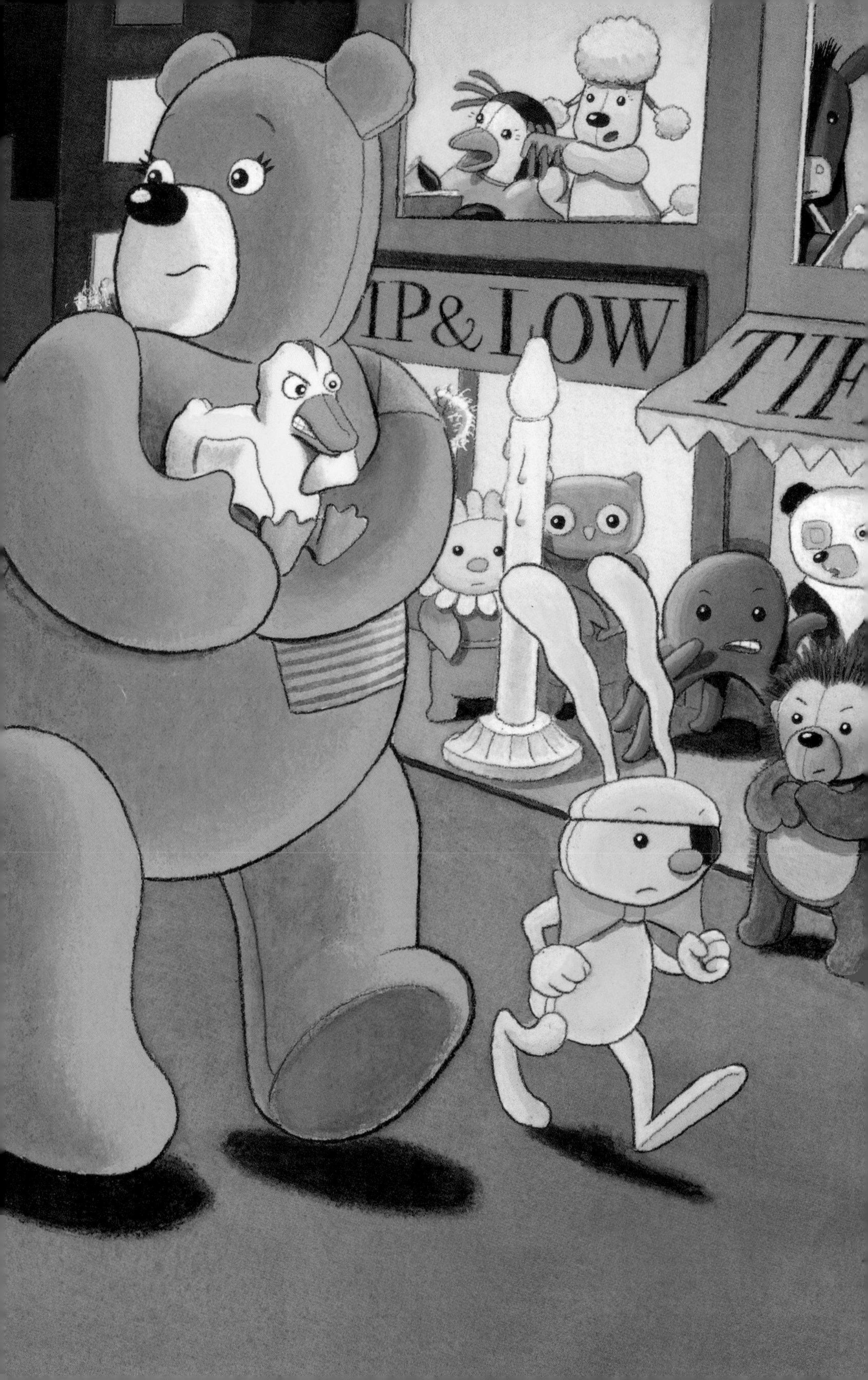
IP&LOW

"Try not to attract attention," I whispered. But it seems Duckie had his own ideas about the situation. I had just gotten the words out of my mouth when the duck leaps from Big Stuff's arms and starts madly chasin' a caramel-colored bulldog.

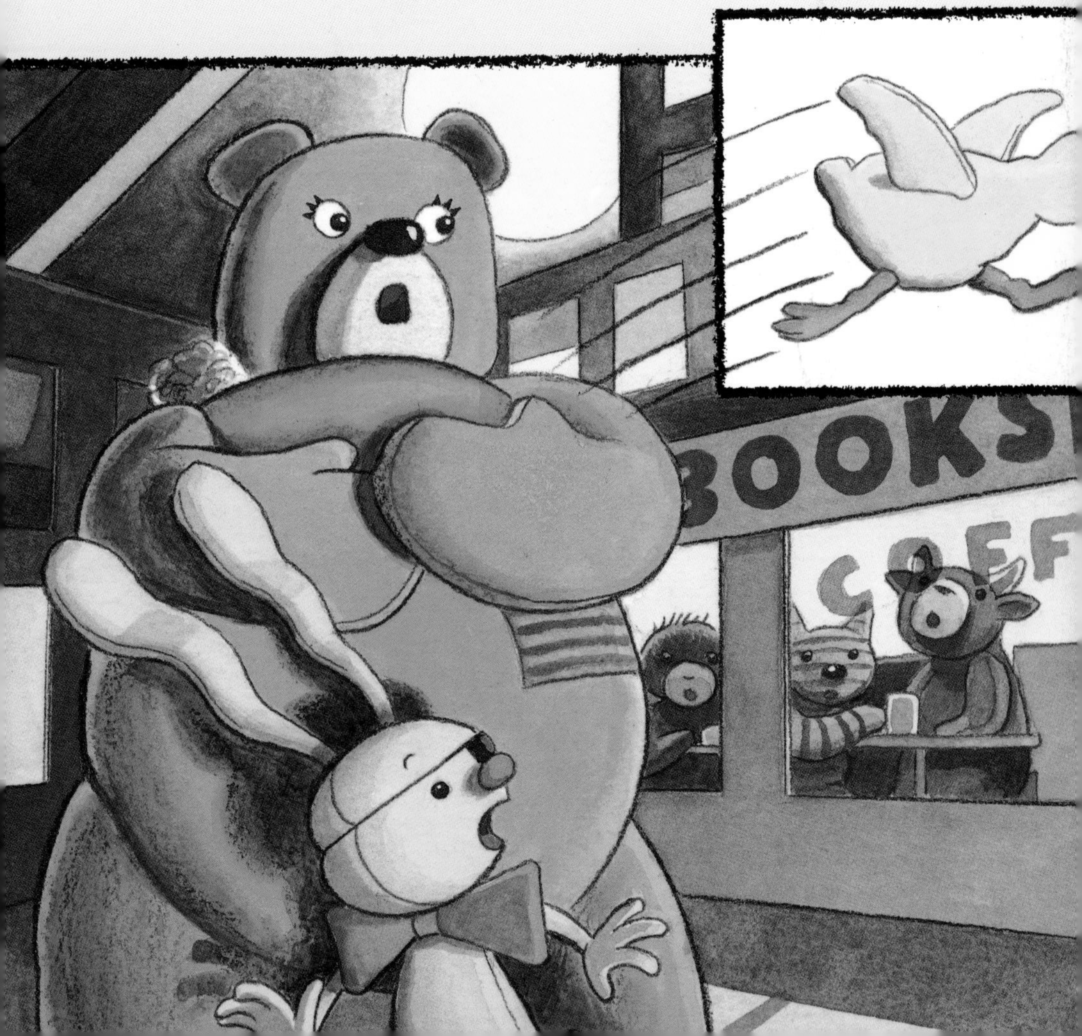

The dog barked a familiar "YIKE!

YIKE! YIKE!"

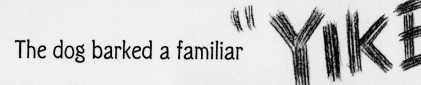

and slipped around the corner out of sight. Duckie followed in hot pursuit.

Soon the dog was back, this time with Duckie's bill clamped to his beanie butt.

"QUERK! QUERK!

QUERRK!"

growled the duck.

"HELP!!!

GET HIM OFF ME!!"

cried the beanbag.

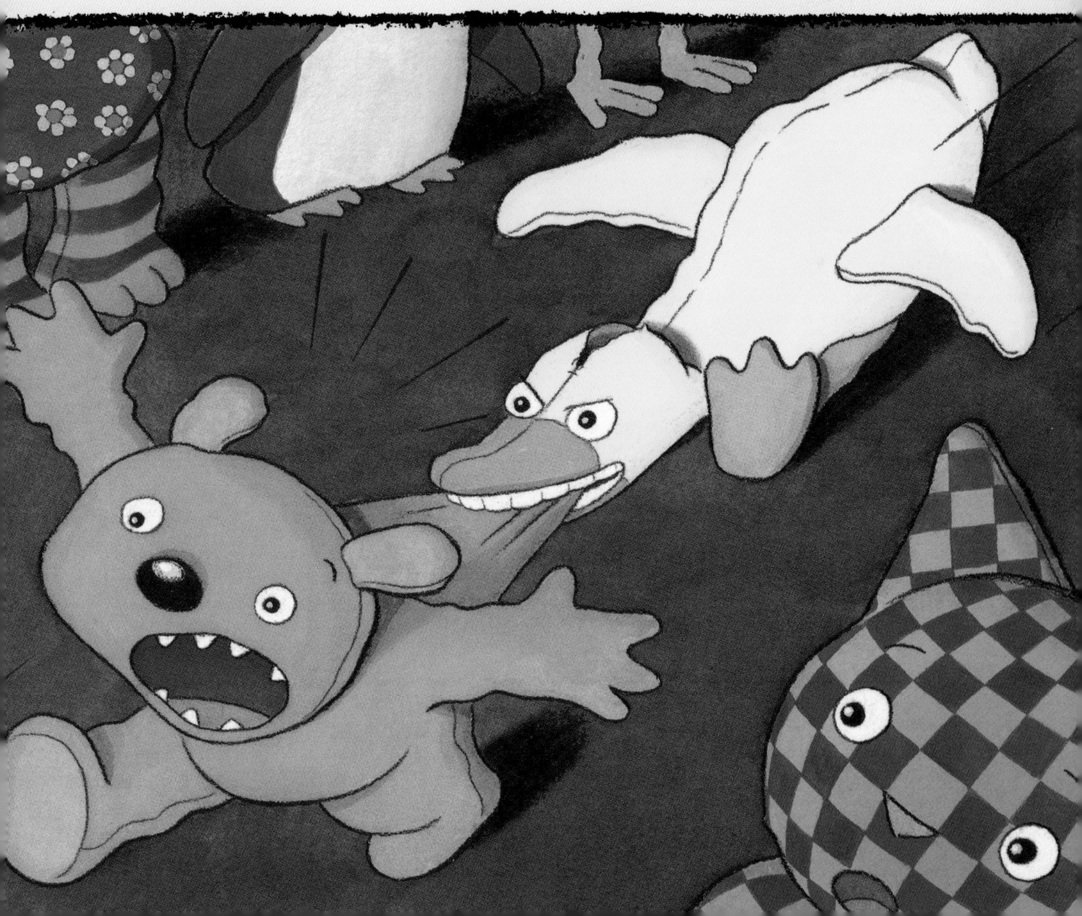

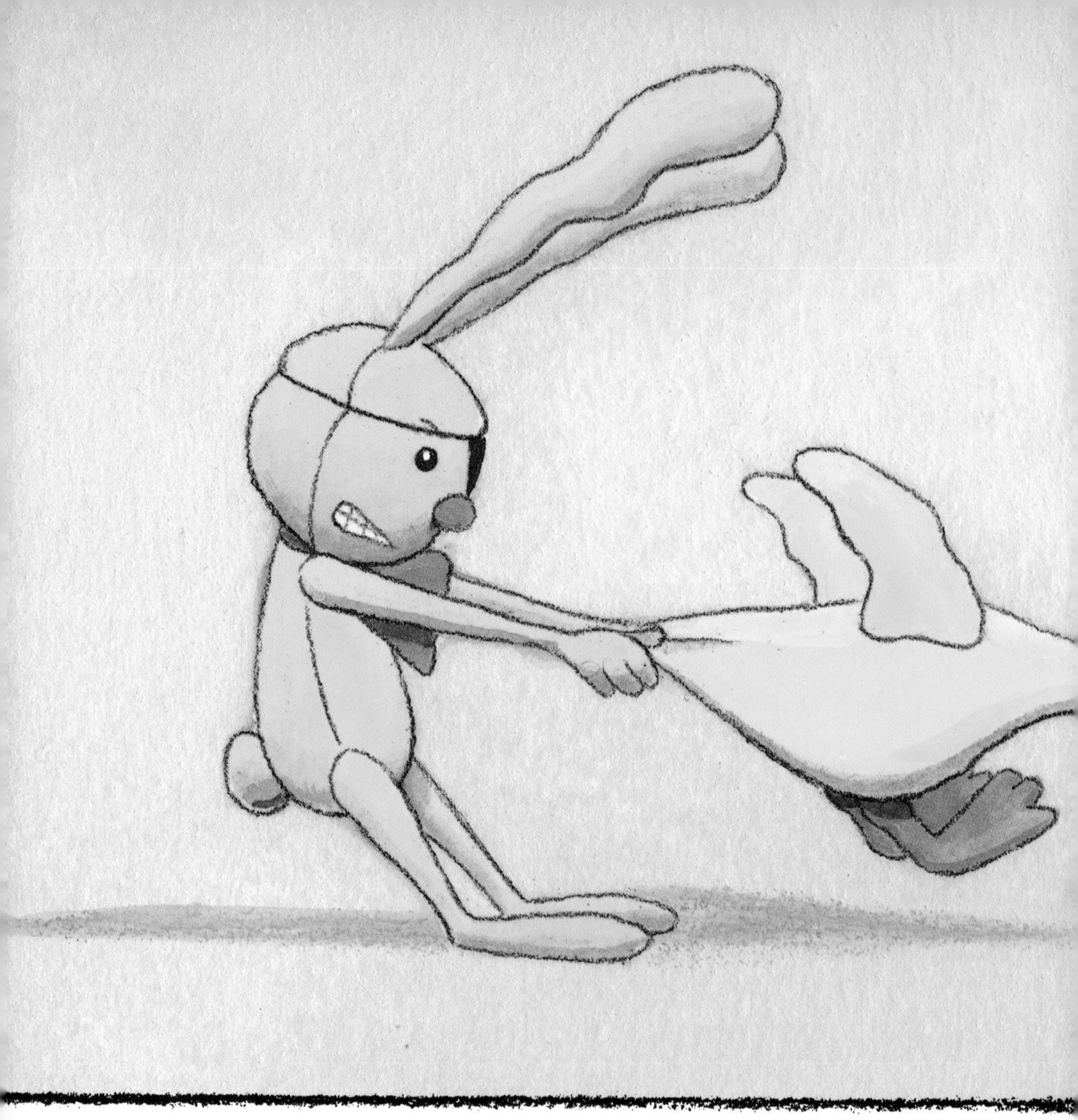

I pried Duckie off of the bulldog's tail, sat him against a street lamp, and looked him in the eye. "Spill it, Beanbag! Where's Duckie's brain!?"

"I don't know!" the beandog whined.

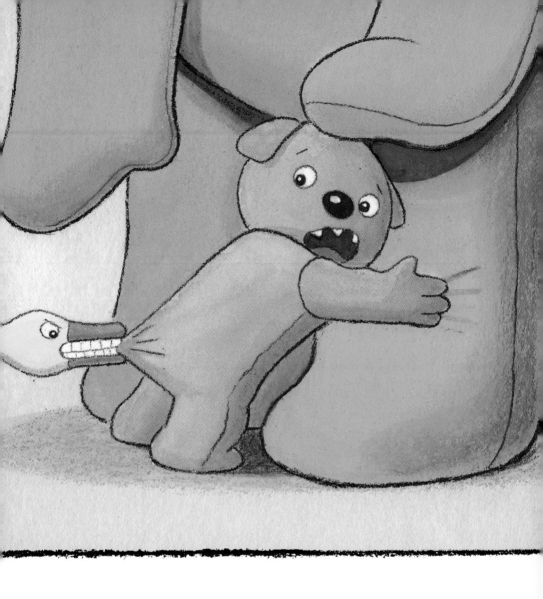

"I don't even know what a duck brain looks like!"

I had no idea what a duck brain looked like either, but it wasn't a pretty thought, so I changed the subject.

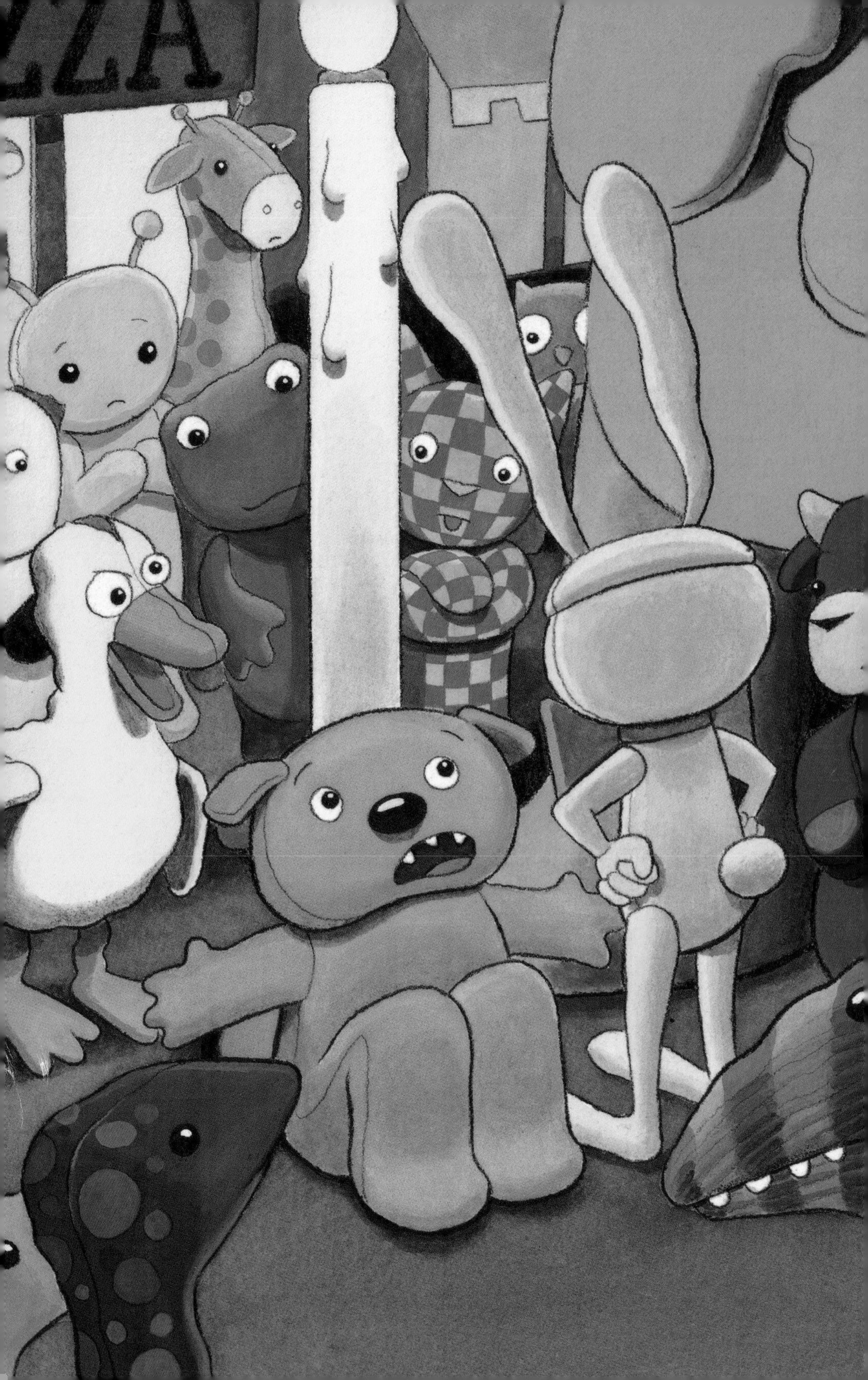

"All right then, why were you sneakin'
around Duckie's apartment?"

"We were just lookin' for the stories!"
he whined.

"We?" I looked up to find the whole street
crawlin' with beanbags! They came in all styles
and editions: polka-dotted cats, striped fish,
paisley insects, chenille lizards. There was even a
cute little flowered rabbit.

"How about you tell me your story?" I said to
the beandog. "And start at the beginning."

The bulldog, known as Butterbean, then told
me that he and the rest of the beanbags used
to listen in secret whenever Duckie was readin'
to Big Stuff.

"Every night the big bear here would show up at Duckie's place and stick her head in the top window. At first we were just curious about the bear, but then we heard the stories. . . ."

"Mooving tales!" lowed a beancow.

"Such powerful oration!" an owl reminisced.

"So," I said, "you were all hidin' out, listenin' to Duckie read. What next?"

"Well, that's about it. Then one night, we were listenin' in when all of a sudden, Duckie, he just stopped readin' and started quackin'. When he wouldn't stop, the big blue bear started actin' crazy. We got scared, so we ran away."

"You're quite a storyteller yourself," I said to the dog, as I helped him up. "You wouldn't happen to remember the title of the book Duckie was readin' that night, would ya?"

A kitten beanbag piped up and said, "It was about pirates!"

"TrrrrrEASURE!" burped a frog.

"The high seas!" said a fish.

"Polly urgently needed a cracker," a parrot remembered.

"Hmmmm." I looked up at Big Stuff and winked. "I think we're close to solvin' this case," I said. "Let's go back to Duckie's place."

I turned to Butterbean. "You better come with us. Oh, and by the way, I believe this is yours," I said, as I handed him the bean from my pocket.

BACK TO DUCKIE'S

We hightailed it back to Duckie's apartment. There on the table, right where we had left it, was the book, *The High-Seas Adventures of Blue Jay the Pirate.*

I flipped through the book until I came to a chapter with the title, "In Which a Parrot Is Rescued from Certain Starvation." There, between pages forty-four and forty-five, was a wad of flattened fluff. "Behold!" I announced. "Duckie's brain!"

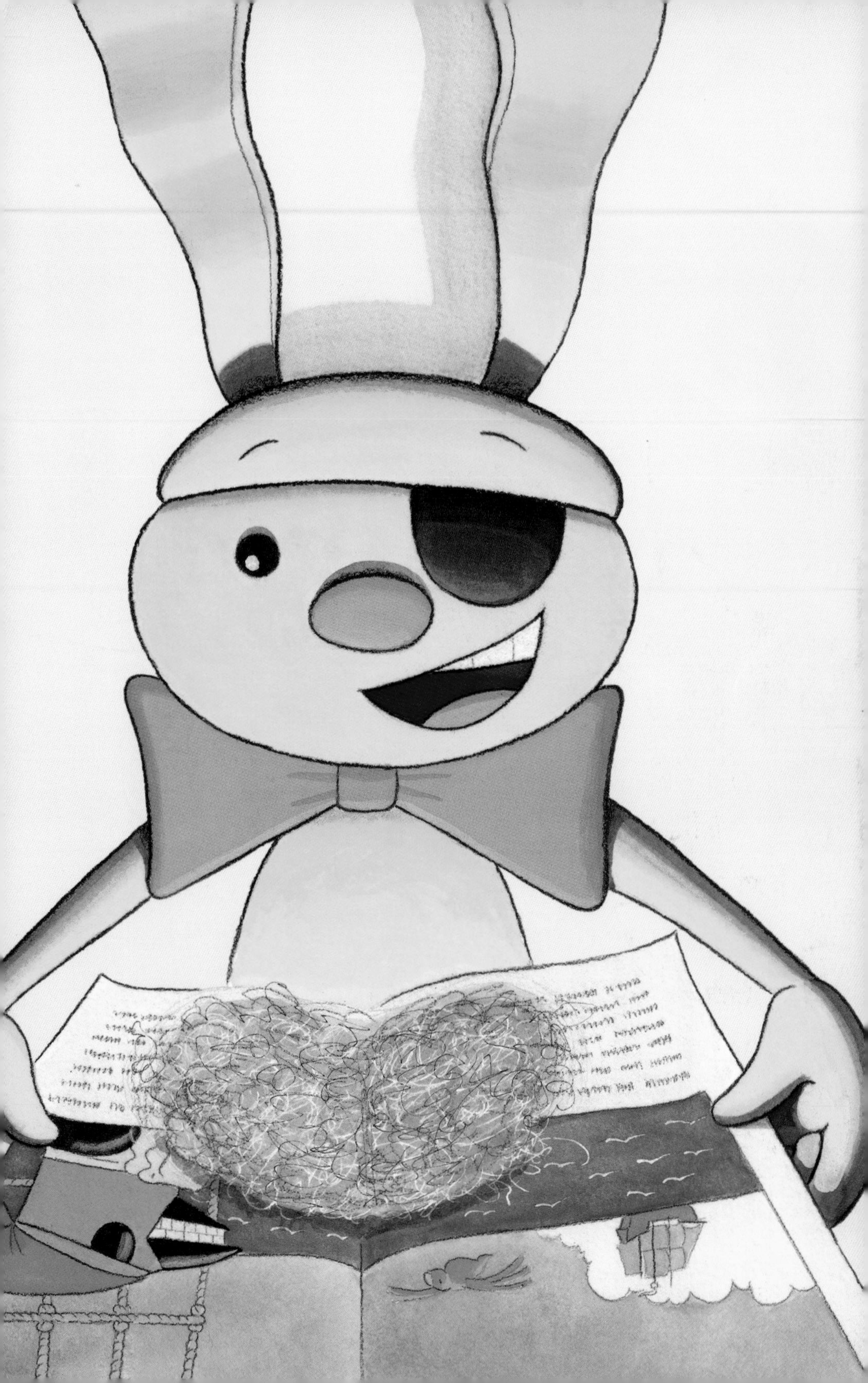

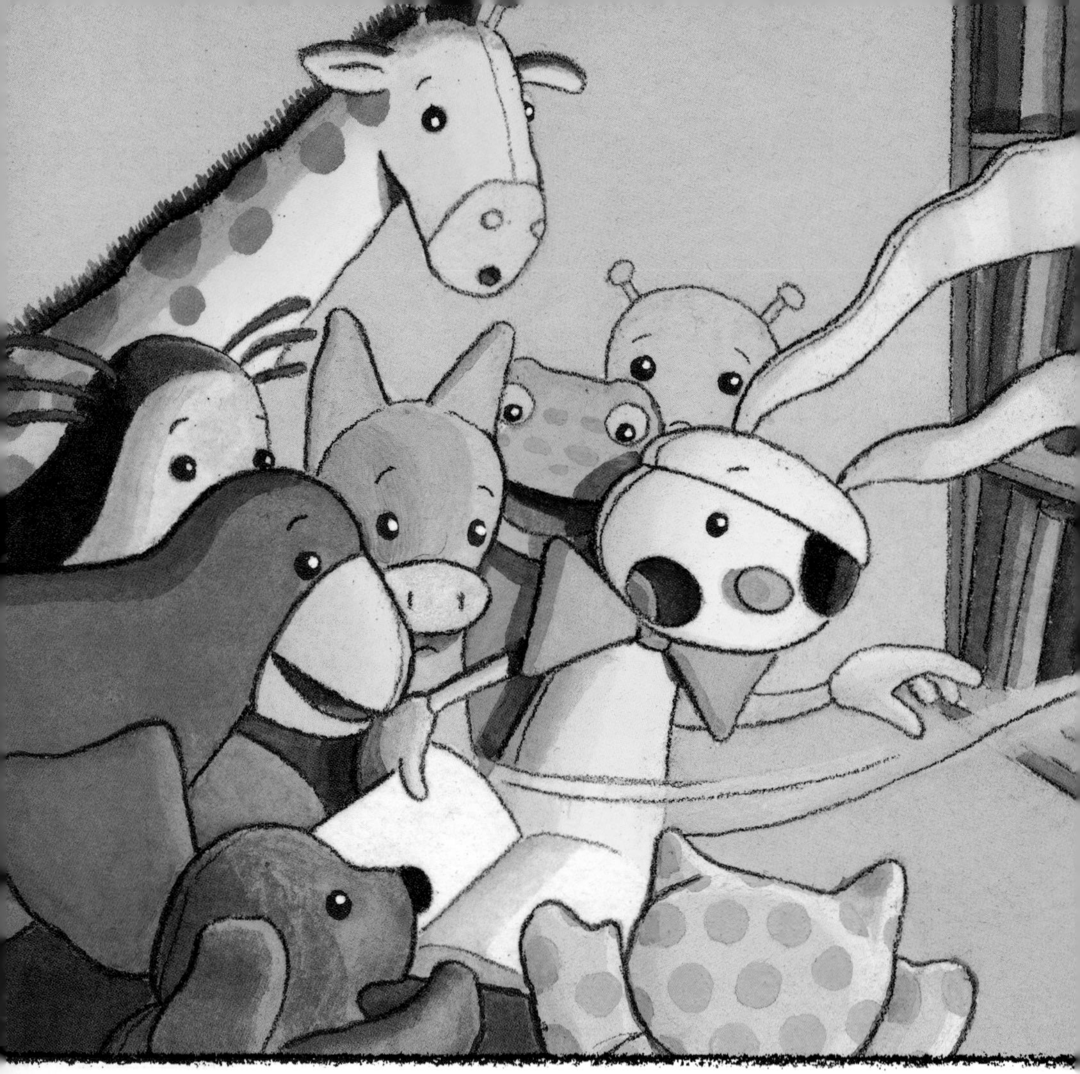

Everyone rushed to see. “Stand back!” I hollered.

But it was too late. The gust of air caused by the surge of onlookers made Duckie’s fluffy brain shoot straight out of the book and into Big Stuff’s gaping mouth!

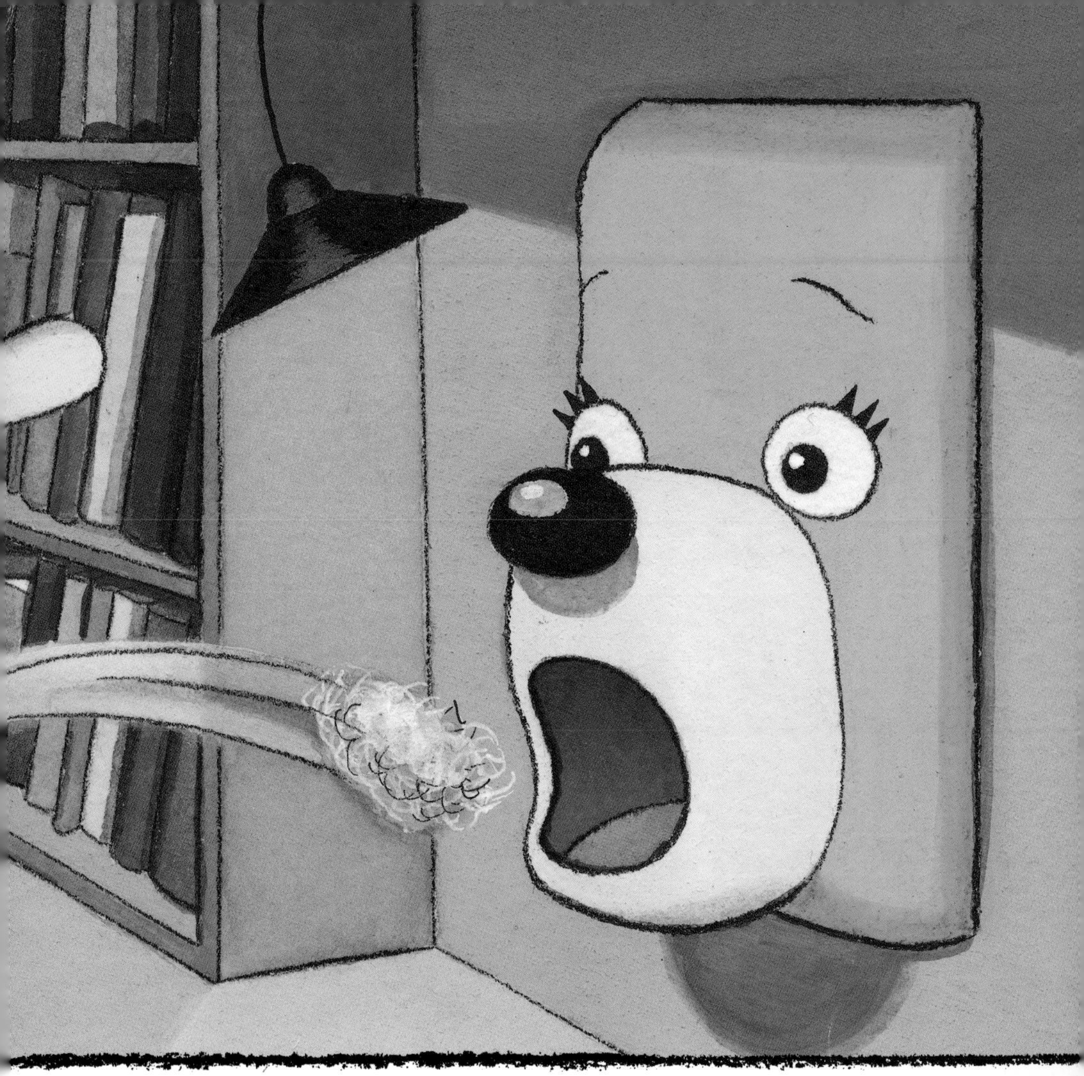

Big Stuff turned green and tried to cough it up. But soon we had to face facts: Duckie's brain was gone for good.

"QUAFFED!" squeaked Duckie weakly, and he crumpled to the floor.

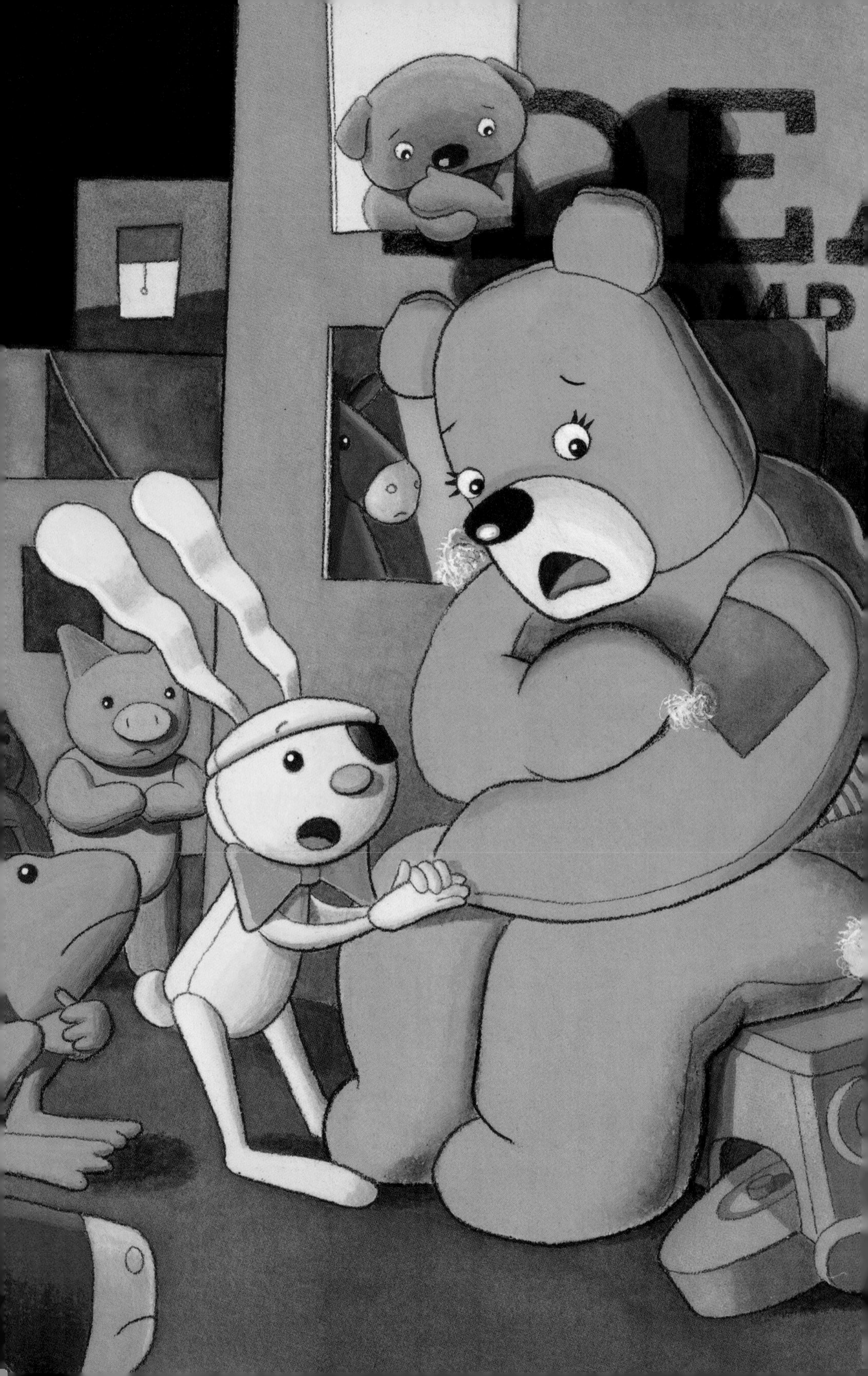

"I feel queasy!" Big Stuff looked as if she was gonna faint.

"It's okay, sweetheart. You'll be all right. Just have a seat and put your head down."

I have to admit, I was stumped. I didn't know what to do next. For a long minute I stood there and watched Big Stuff forlornly pickin' at the fluff pokin' out of the holes in her threadbare fur.

"Fluff! That's it!" I shouted. "Butterbean, stay here with Duckie. I'll be right back!" I said, as I ran out the door.

Down on the street I said, "Big Stuff, I have a crazy idea that might save Duckie, but I need your help."

"Oh Tuff, I'd do anything for that little fuzzy guy!" she cried.

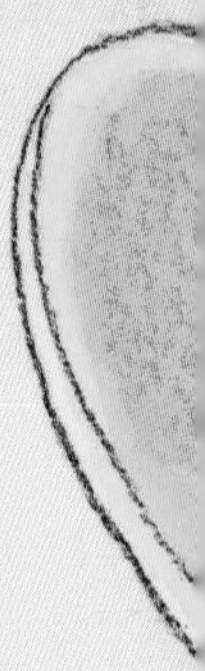

"Okay," I said, and took a deep breath. "Maybe all Duckie needs is some of your extra fluff."

Big Stuff smiled, stood up slowly, and gently pulled tufts of stuffing from wherever she could find it until we had a big ball of fluff.

"Stand clear," I ordered, and I carried the precious stuff up the stairs to the apartment, where Duckie was still out cold.

Butterbean and I attempted a rare and risky operation—a brain transplant in a stuffed duck.

"I need hot water, clean towels, a tray, and a spoon!" Butterbean said to the beanbags assisting us.

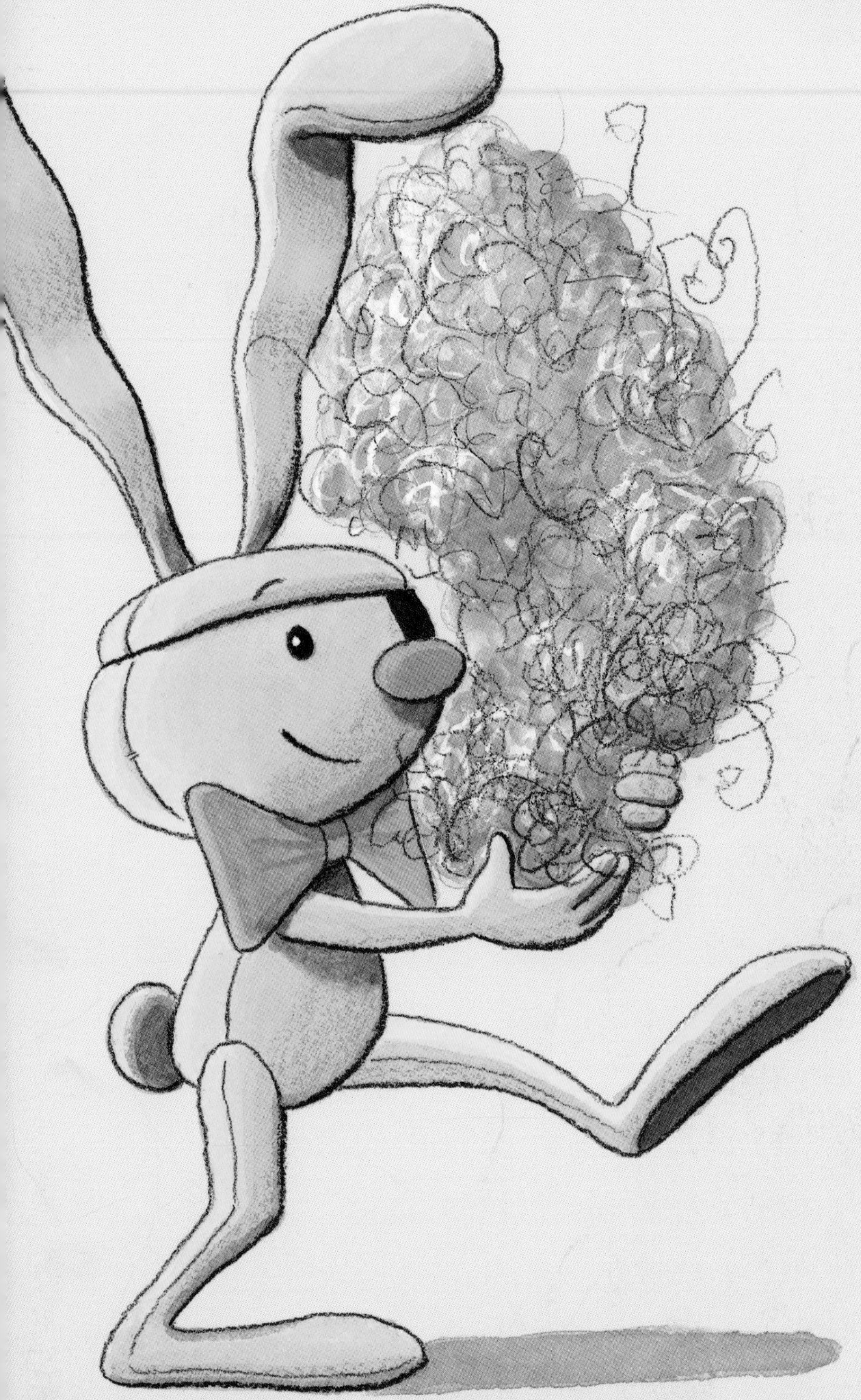

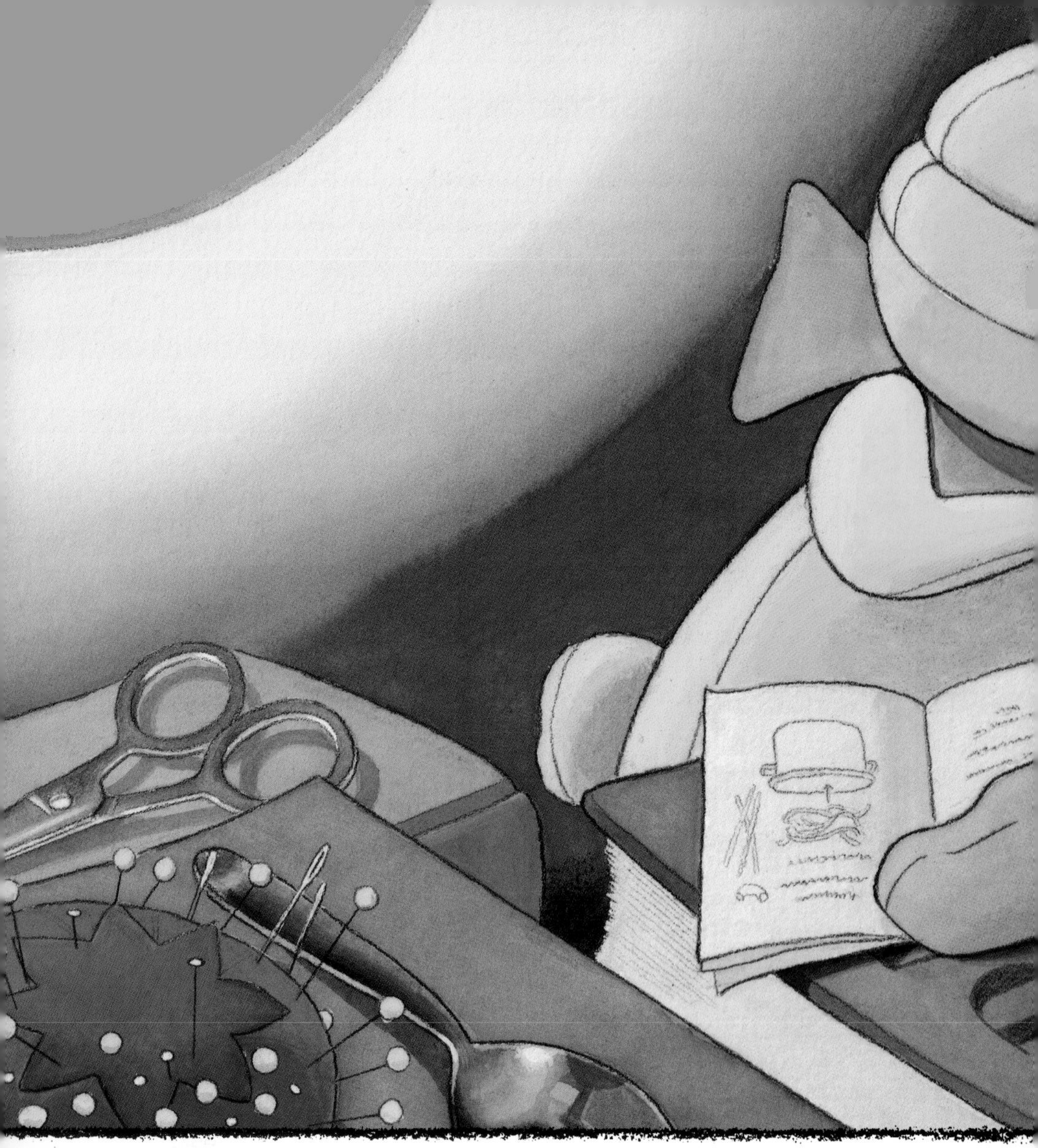

The two of us prepped for surgery. I carefully set down the ball of fluff. Butterbean surprised me by placing his bean next to the fluff on the tray.

"What's with this?" I says.

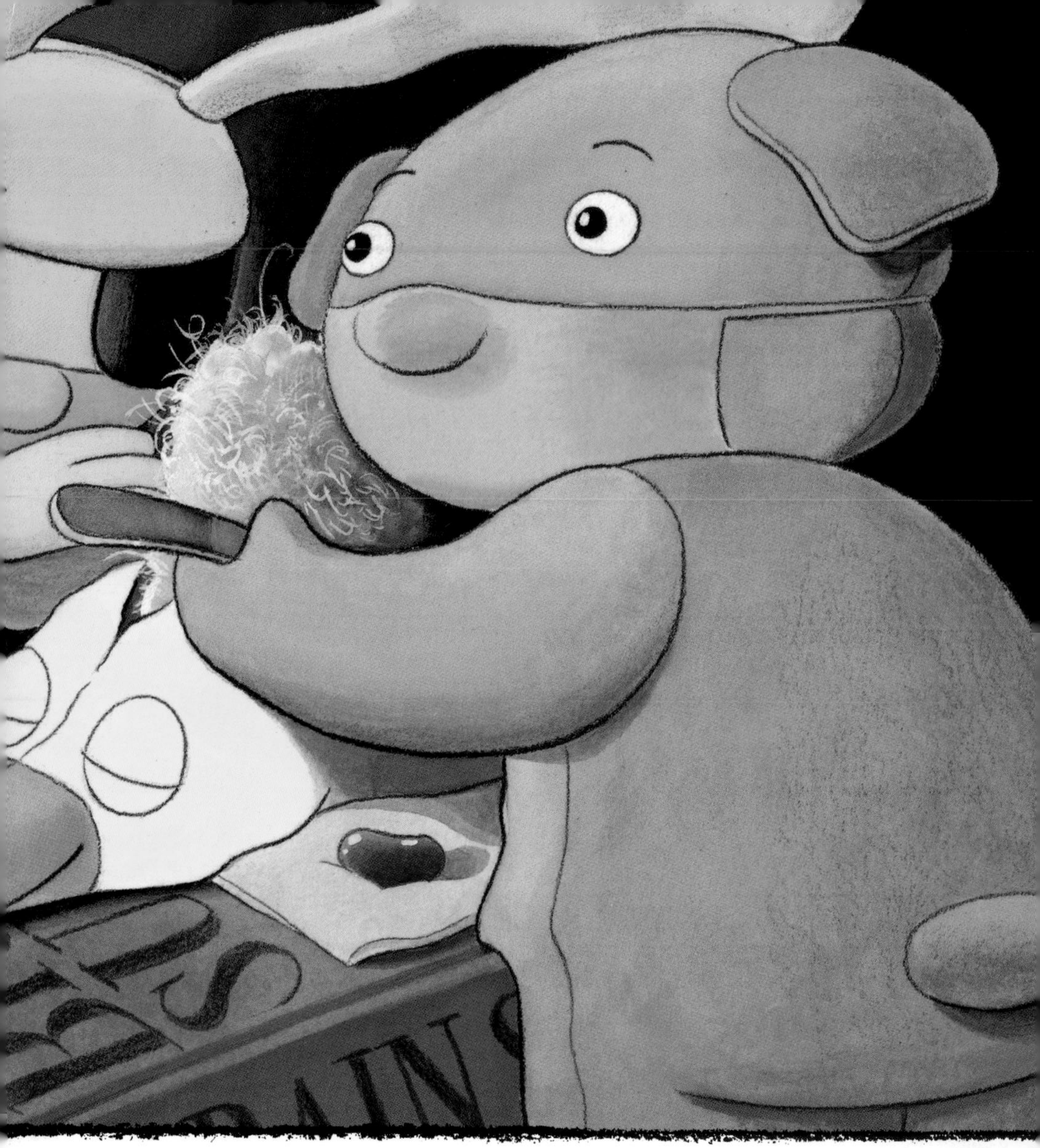

Butterbean solemnly explained, “Duckie is part beanbag to us. Our brains are beans. This might help.”

So we filled Duckie’s head with a bunch of fluff and a bean.

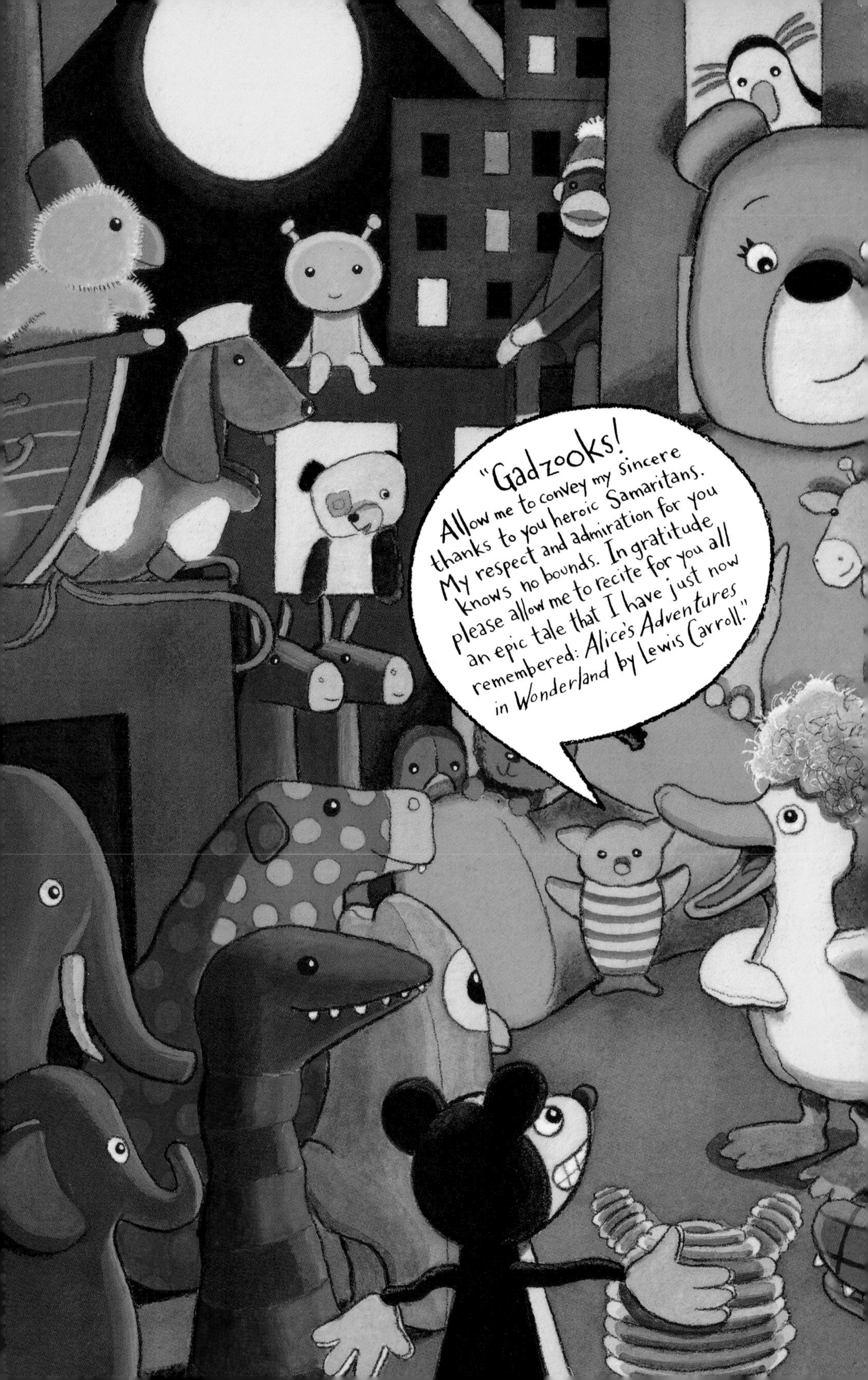
"Gadzooks! Allow me to convey my sincere thanks to you heroic Samaritans. My respect and admiration for you knows no bounds. In gratitude please allow me to recite for you all an epic tale that I have just now remembered: *Alice's Adventures in Wonderland* by Lewis Carroll."

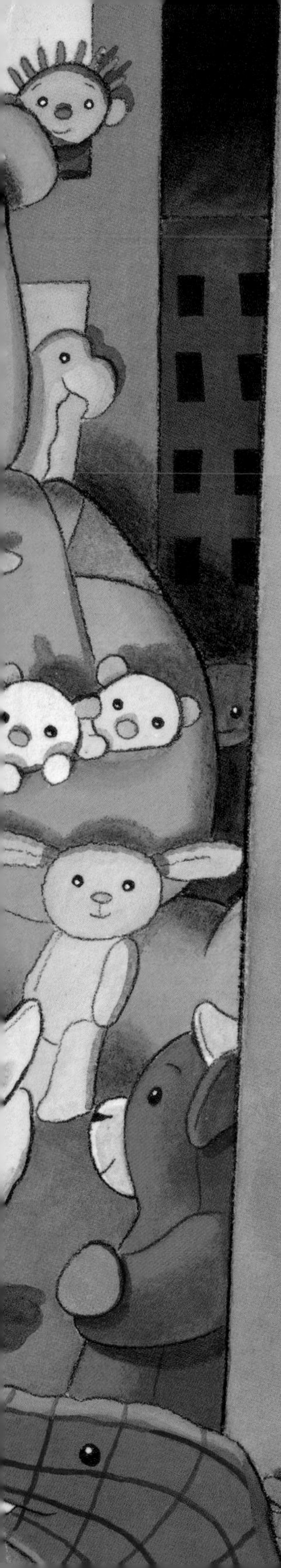

It wasn't pretty, but it worked like a charm. Smarter than ever, Duckie began to tell stories to an adoring audience of stuffs, bean-bags, and one very happy, slightly slimmer Bluebell.

As for me, I only stayed for the beginnin' of the first chapter. Before I left, though, I got a hot tip for my crossword from that dexterous duck. "Duckie! What's an eight-letter word for *fake medicine*?"

Duckie smiled a mile and said, "My dear Tuff, that would be

quackery!"

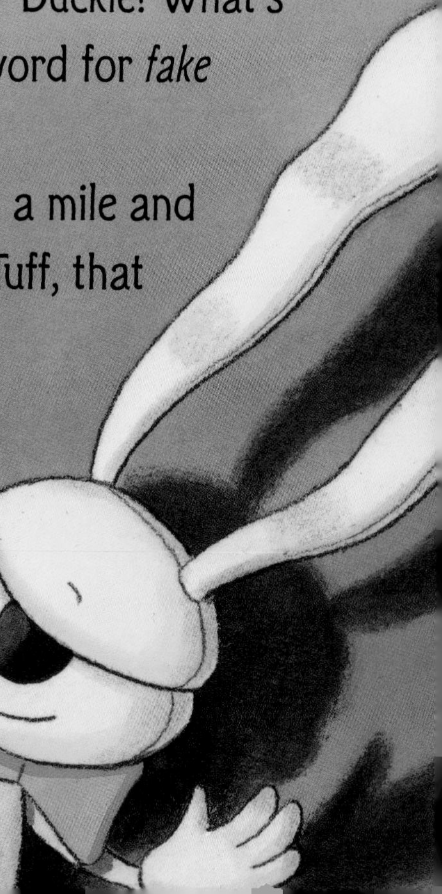

3:29 A.M.
as usual

CASE CLOSED

I walked the empty street back to my office, sat down at the desk, and filled in the last word to complete the crossword puzzle.

I leaned back in my chair and looked at the clock: 3:29, as usual. It was a quiet night in a new city where beanbags and stuffs sat side by side, listening to stories.

Meanwhile, I'm in La-La Land, dreamin' up my own stories, starrin' Tuff Fluff, rabbit detective, and his two partners, Duckie and Bluebell, a.k.a. Smart Fluff and Big Fluff.

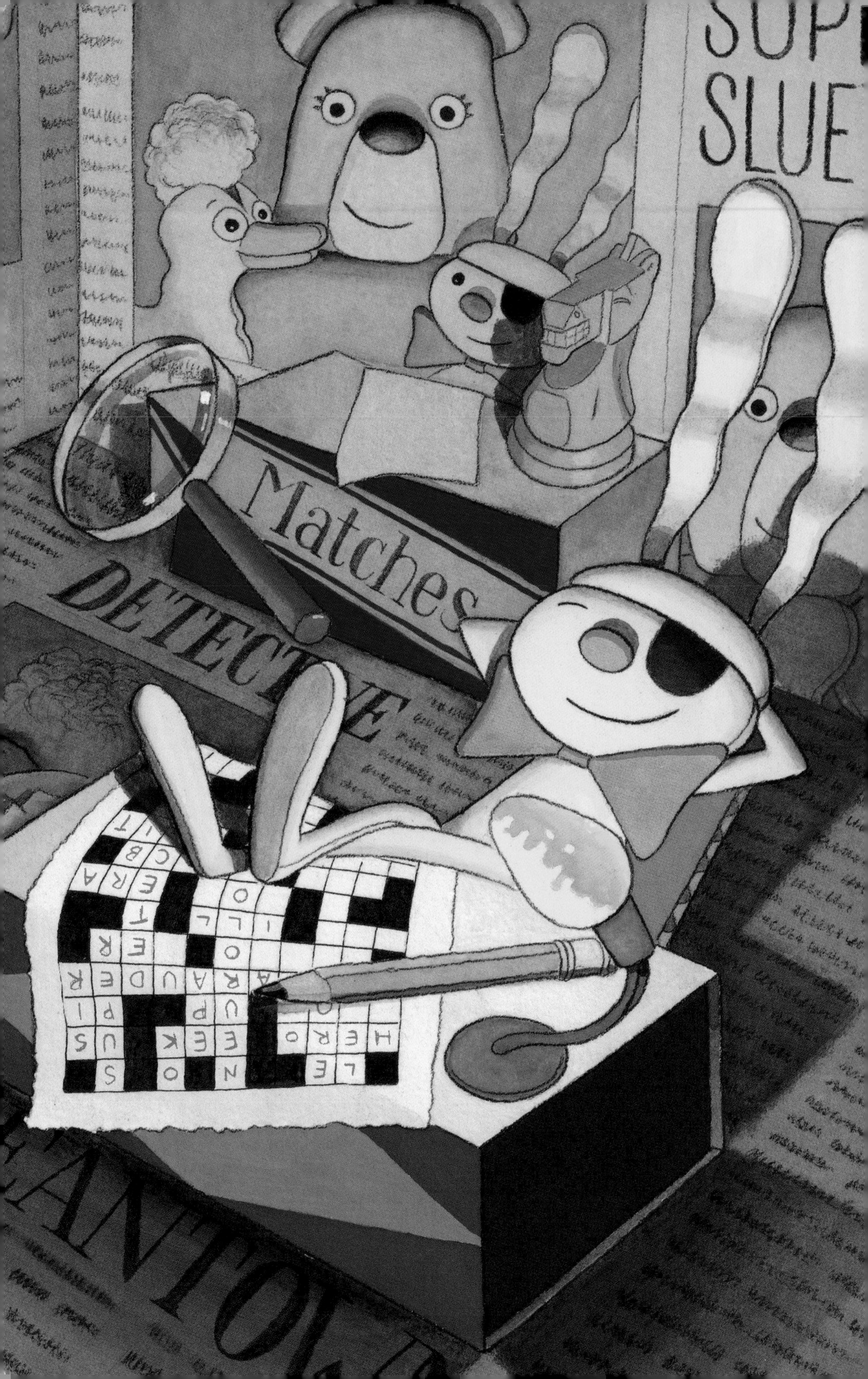
SUP
SLUE
Matches

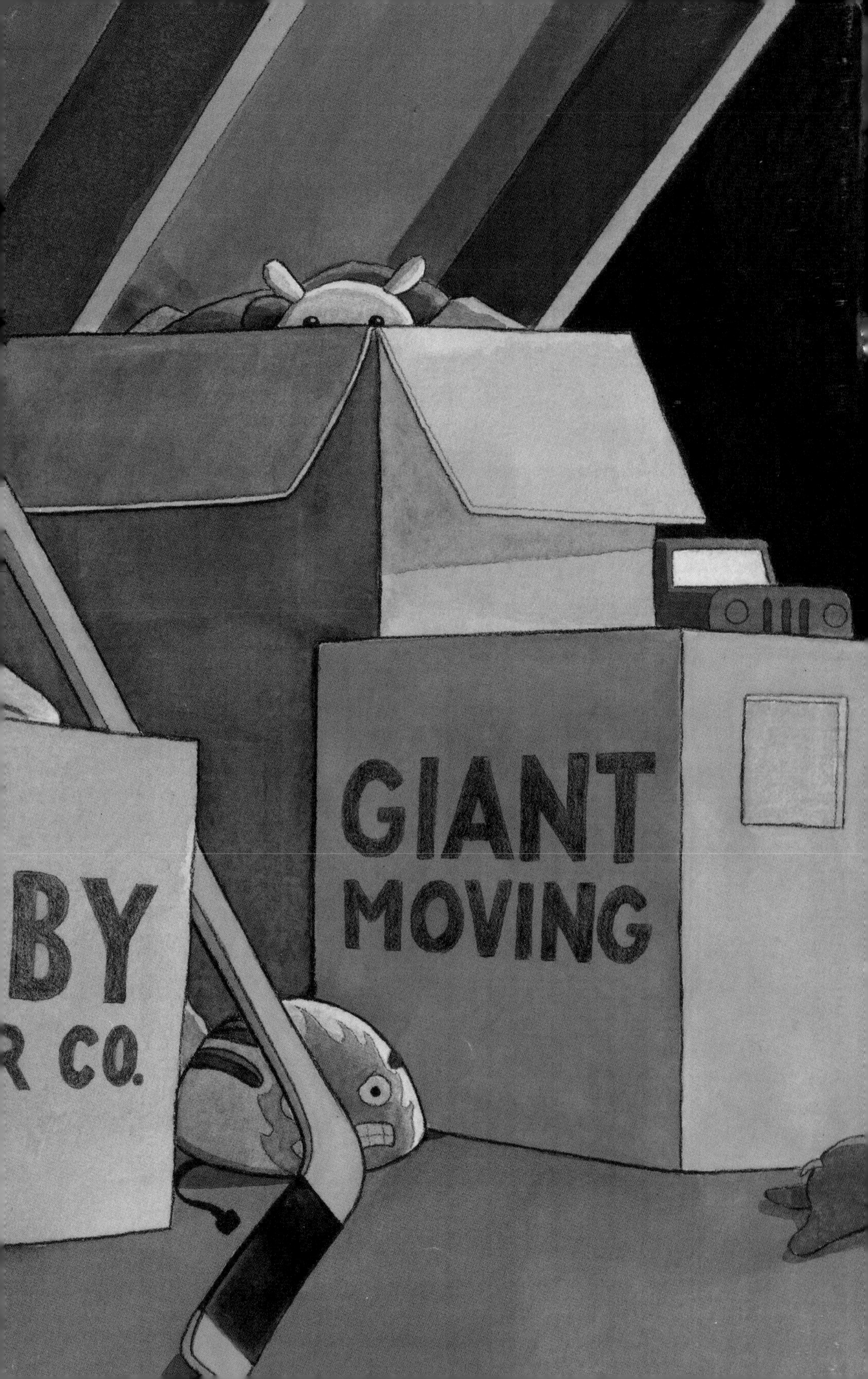
GIANT
MOVING
BY
R CO.